SET
YOU
FREE

SET YOU FREE

JEFF ROSS

ORCA BOOK PUBLISHERS

Library and Archives Canada Cataloguing in Publication

Ross, Jeff, 1973-, author
Set you free / Jeff Ross.

Issued in print and electronic formats.
ISBN 978-1-4598-0797-6 (pbk.).—ISBN 978-1-4598-0798-3 (pdf).—
ISBN 978-1-4598-0799-0 (epub)

I. Title.
PS8635.06928S48 2015   jc813'.6   c2015-901718-1
c2015-901719-x

First published in the United States, 2015
Library of Congress Control Number: 2015935525

Summary: In this YA thriller, Lauren's brother becomes a suspect in a child's
disappearance, and Lauren teams up with a computer enthusiast to uncover the truth.

Orca Book Publishers is dedicated to preserving the environment and has printed this book on
Forest Stewardship Council® certified paper.

Orca Book Publishers gratefully acknowledges the support for its publishing
programs provided by the following agencies: the Government of Canada through
the Canada Book Fund and the Canada Council for the Arts, and the Province of British
Columbia through the BC Arts Council and the Book Publishing Tax Credit.

Design by Rachel Page
Cover images by Getty Images, Shutterstock and Dreamstime
Author photo by David Irvine

ORCA BOOK PUBLISHERS
www.orcabook.com

Printed and bound in Canada.

18   17   16   15   •   4   3   2   1

*For Alex and Luca—you might not always be
best friends, but you'll always be brothers.
And Megan, always.*

ONE

SUNDAY

Family should always come first.

Right?

I mean, you can fight with your siblings. You can argue with your parents. You can call one another idiots, but if an outsider says one bad word about any member of your family, it's war.

That's the way it's supposed to be.

But how often is this true? How often do we let our family members drift, fall into their own pains and troubles, then disappear completely?

I'd like to say I always stood up for my brother. I'd also like to say that one day I will repay him for how I used to treat him. But I can't make that promise. I wish I could. But no one knows what the future holds.

And the past is unchangeable. What we have is the present. And this morning my present is painful.

My head aches. My stomach rolls. My mouth feels filled with cotton balls.

And then this: "Lauren, honey. There's a police officer here who would like to speak with you."

"Why?" I say to my mother. Disaster videos stream through my muddled mind. Friends in burned-out, smashed-up cars.

"Ben Carter is missing."

"Two minutes," I say, swinging my feet out of the bed and cradling my head. "Give me two minutes."

— — — —

Ben Carter is my final babysitting charge. I'm seventeen and I've been done with babysitting for a few years, but I haven't let go of Ben.

I was with him yesterday until five o'clock. I mostly only see him on the weekends now, while his mother, Erin, volunteers at the hospital. Erin's mother was well cared for there before she died last year, and volunteering is Erin's way to give back, I guess.

And then Ben was home with his family, and I did what I always do on Saturday nights.

I went to a party.

I hung out.

I drank.

If I'm being honest with myself, which rarely happens these days, I'm not even sure I like drinking. I make promises to myself every Saturday afternoon.

Stay home tonight.

Watch a movie.

Catch up with an old friend.

Get some homework done.

Then the phone calls come in, and everyone says this party is going to be the biggest, the best, the most exciting event of the year.

Absolutely not to be missed.

Epic.

I bend easily. It's a character flaw. But if there's a choice between going out and seeing what might happen and staying in and knowing what will (nothing), I always take going out.

As I step out the door I make more promises. Go, have fun, talk, dance, drink some water. Tell people you're the designated driver if you have to.

But once I get to the party, someone will convince me that one drink won't hurt. One drink is social. One drink is courteous.

So I have one courteous drink.

But one becomes two, becomes three, becomes…

New promises are made the next day. I'm going to fly straight. Get back to my old world, where I was studious, quiet, unremarkable. I spend hours looking at college brochures and trying to imagine myself sitting in a lecture hall, inhaling ideas. But the next step is not there. The "what happens after college" step. The "what do you want to do with your life" step.

I have no idea.

And that terrifies me.

So I try to get back to studying. I try to be good and hardworking, but as far as I can tell, the world does not want me to be good and hardworking.

It wants me to mix with the right people, say the right things.

Go to the right parties.

Drink.

Last night's jeans are in a twisty, gross ball on the floor. My favorite sweatshirt is at the end of my bed, now sporting a long green stain and a torn cuff.

I grab my glasses off the side table. The eyeball fairy must have taken pity on me last night, because my eyes aren't burning from leaving my contacts in.

I go to my closet and pull out the first things I touch: capris and a T-shirt.

I push my hair around without looking in the mirror. I feel like garbage. Smell worse.

Whatever.

Off to talk to Mr. Policeman.

TWO

Or, rather, Ms. Policewoman.

"Detective Carole Evans. Would you care to take a seat?" she asks, pointing at my own couch.

Like she owns the place.

She's taller than me, with light-blue eyes and too-tweezed eyebrows. No makeup. Her face looks undefined, as if her features have been flung onto a blank canvas and left to their own devices.

She's wearing a black button-down blouse and tight gray pants. Nike running shoes and a wedding ring. As I'm sitting down, she says, "Would you mind if I asked you what happened to that eye?"

Which is a way of asking, isn't it.

"What?" I put my hand beneath my glasses.

"Something hit you?"

I go to the mirror. In the bright light it looks as if I've recently been crying: there are streaks on my cheeks cutting rivers through a dusting of dirt.

My hands are filthy.

What went on last night?

Right, the bonfire. I close my eyes as visions of the beach at night return like scenes cut from an otherwise all-right movie.

I touch the bruise. It feels like an undercooked steak. There's a tiny cut to the left of my right eye.

"I can't believe it got that bad," I say, turning around. "It was a stupid accident. Last night I opened a car door, and then my friend Stacy said something to me. I turned and said, like, *one minute* or whatever, and when I turned back someone had opened the door a little more, and I smacked right into it."

"On the top corner?" Detective Evans says.

"Exactly. It didn't look like anything last night, but it sure does now."

I sit on the couch and try to change the subject before Detective Evans can conjure any more questions regarding my social life. "I'll be fine. So what's happened to Ben?"

Detective Evans pulls out a notebook. "You were with Benjamin Carter yesterday, correct?"

"All day," I say. "What's happened?"

"All we know at the moment is that his mother put him to bed last night, and this morning he was gone."

6

"Gone?" I say. "Where would he go? He's five years old."

"We don't know, Lauren. That's why I'm here."

"Okay," I say, because what do I know about these things? The Carters live two blocks away, and nothing really bad ever happens in our area. It's the suburbs! People come here to get away from bad things.

"Have you seen him today?" Detective Evans asks.

I push at my hair, a habit sent down through our DNA from mother to daughter for generations. It's a miracle that we all aren't bald. "I just woke up," I say. "I dropped him off yesterday at around five, if that's any help."

"How did Benjamin seem yesterday?"

"Normal?" I offer.

"Did he say anything about running away?"

"No," I say. "He's never said anything like that."

"Did he seem sad or upset at all?"

"No." I realize I'm endlessly shaking my head no and put a stop to it. "We played in the park, had ice cream. He kept talking about these things called Beyblades."

"You mean the little tops that ram into one another?"

"Yeah, those."

"What was he saying about them?"

"Just that he wanted a couple of new ones and his mother wouldn't get them for him. But that happens a lot. He's five—he wants everything."

"Was there a particular reason his mother wouldn't get them for him?"

"Do you mean because they might be violent or dangerous or something?"

"I suppose."

"No. Like you said, they're just tops that ram against one another."

Detective Evans stares at me, and I decide to fill the silence. "They all have different names and abilities. Some are attack and others are defense. So you have to decide what kind of battle you're having and choose the right top."

"Did you notice anything at all out of the ordinary with Benjamin?" she asks.

"He was the same old Benny."

"How about Erin? Did you notice anything different with her?"

"Not that I can think of. She spent the day volunteering at the hospital."

Detective Evans flips a page in her notebook, then flips it right back again. "Did you happen to see any other members of the Carter family yesterday?"

"Not while I was with Ben, no."

"But after?"

I glance at my mother, who is sitting on the edge of a chair. She has always given me a certain amount of freedom, and though I normally am good about respecting it, I know I've stepped beyond my bounds recently. I mean, if she knew

I was out drinking, she'd lose her mind. But she gets these horrible migraines that sometimes put her out for days. So she mostly doesn't have a choice but to trust me.

"There was a bonfire last night, and Ben's stepbrother and stepsister were both there," I say quickly. My mother doesn't react to this. I guess she is focused on the fact that Ben is missing.

"Jack Junior and Stephanie."

"People call him JJ."

"Did you speak to them at all about Benjamin?"

"I didn't speak to them about anything," I say.

"Did you notice when they left the bonfire?"

I adjust my glasses, remembering why I hate wearing them. I can't leave them alone and am always pushing them back up my nose. "No, there were a lot of people there. I saw JJ and Steph, but that was it. We don't really hang out."

"What about Benjamin's father, Jack Carter? Did you see or speak to him yesterday?"

"He was at an event, I think."

"The mayor is a busy man," Detective Evans says, still creeping me out with her penetrating stare. I feel like a problem she has to solve. Like she's been a cop so long that people are no different than paperwork to her. Something you read, scribble on, then either pass along or file away.

"Do you think you can help us today, Lauren?" she says.

"How?"

"I'd like to visit all the places you were with Benjamin yesterday. If he's run off, we'll possibly find him somewhere he's recently been. Would that be okay?"

I say, "Could I get something to eat first?"

"I can make you some breakfast," Mom says.

Detective Evans stands and pockets her notepad. "Let me buy you something on the road. The sooner we get going, the better. If that is okay with you, Mrs. Saunders."

"She wouldn't want to be a bother," Mom says.

"Do you really think he could have run away?" I say.

Detective Evans is flipping through something on her cell phone. That uncomfortable someone-is-staring-at-their-cell-phone silence occurs. I let it pass, waiting for her to come back to reality. Finally, she looks up. "That's sometimes the case."

"How's his mom doing?" I say. "How is Erin?"

She quickly types something into the phone before finally putting it away. "As well as you might imagine. Same with the mayor."

I grab my purse off the coffee table. "Quick teeth brush," I say.

"I'll meet you in the car."

In the bathroom, I take two extra-strength pain-killers to try to cut the inevitable brain-splitting headache off at the pass. I brush my teeth, wipe the dirt from my face and step into my bedroom. I grab my cell phone from the charger, slide it into my pocket and head out of the bedroom and to the front door. I stop for a second there, looking outside. My temples are pulsing. I feel incredibly dehydrated.

My teeth ache.

I close my eyes and attempt to focus. Try to remember the night before. The afternoon with Benny. But everything is a blur.

You have to wonder about humans sometimes. The things we do to ourselves in the name of entertainment. Or because what seems like fun is really just what everyone else is doing, and our lack of imagination and courage makes us all followers.

When I come back out, my mother has disappeared into the kitchen.

"I'm leaving, Mom," I yell.

"You'll find him," she calls back. "He can't have gone far."

"It'll be okay," I say.

I inhale one last deep breath and step outside.

THREE

The street outside the Carters' is packed with cars. We slow as we pass, then keep going toward Ravine Road.

Detective Evans is typing on the in-car laptop as she drives, which seems totally hypocritical because if I got caught glancing at a text while driving, I'd be hit with a giant fine. The radio is streaming a monotone voice saying pretty much only numbers: "85 25 76 15 Hillside. A 5420 Beach and Main. Unit 6509, please respond."

"We should go backward," Detective Evans says, finally focusing on the road. "Start at the end of the day and move to the beginning."

"Okay," I say.

"Unless you can think of somewhere specific Benjamin might have gone."

"I can't," I say.

"Drive-through all right with you?" Detective Evans asks, pointing at the local McDonald's.

"For sure. Thank you." The windows are down, and the early-morning air works at further tangling my hair.

Detective Evans glances at me. "I hear bacon is good the morning after."

"The morning after?" I say, probably too innocently.

"I used to go to bonfires too," she says as we pull into the line. I have no idea how to respond to this, so I spend my mental energy trying to will the car in front of us to move forward.

I get something that looks more like a picture of a bacon-and-egg sandwich than actual food. Two large coffees fit into the cup holders. A side of bacon and home fries. The girl at the drive-through window, Amanda something, whom I've seen around school but don't really know, is eyeing me up. Her thumbs are probably already sending word out to the social stratosphere regarding her new discovery: *Just saw Lauren S in POLICE CAR. WTF? + glasses?*

Tweeted, Facebooked, texted to an inner circle. No picture, though, so POINH, Amanda something. My word against yours.

"Which park did you take Benjamin to?" Detective Evans says.

"The one off Helpern." We're back on the street and moving swiftly around the few early-Sunday vehicles.

"Tell me about him."

"Benny?"

"Yes."

"Well, he's five," I say, taking a first squishy bite of the egg sandwich. "He's—"

"I know that stuff. He's five, weighs sixty-five pounds. Hair brown, eyes brown, last seen wearing Thomas the Tank Engine pajamas. I got all that. But what is he like?"

"He's a good kid. A lot of fun. He's interested in everything. He's always asking questions, trying to figure the world out."

Detective Evans takes a gulp of her coffee. As she's putting the cup back in its holder, she says, "You're seventeen, right?"

"My birthday was last week." I think about the party. It wasn't thrown for me specifically, but some people did bring my favorite drink. And every so often someone would say something like, "Shit, today's your birthday. That's awesome." Stacy got me a giant stuffed penguin named Wobbles. It has these giant, perfectly round eyes, and I carried it around all night, telling everyone how Wobbles was my best friend ever.

"I don't mean to be insulting, but I don't see a lot of seventeen-year-old babysitters."

"I don't sit for anyone else. I've been with Benny since he was one, and it'd be too hard to just never see him again."

"So you've known the family awhile?"

"Mostly Erin. Jack, well, like I said before, he's busy."

Detective Evans says, "A mayor never has a nine-to-five job. Jack's been known to attend three events a night. It's a very difficult career."

She sounds impressed. I've always thought it is crappy for Ben to not have his dad around. It's like you enter politics and your life is no longer your own. You belong to the people, unless, of course, those people are your own family.

"I usually take Benny out," I say. "If it's raining, we go to one of the indoor playgrounds or the library or—"

"What does he like to do?" Detective Evans interrupts.

"I guess what any five-year-old does? He likes the play structure at the park and the swings. We read a lot of books. The Beyblades thing. He just started biking. I think he could get his training wheels off, but Erin's waiting until his dad is around to do that."

"Training wheels is a dad thing for sure. My dad taught me to ride a bike."

"My dad thought it was a better idea to send us out without training wheels and see what happened," I say, immediately wondering why I'm telling her anything about my life. I decide to shut up and look out the window while testing how much coffee I can keep down. Eventually, we pull to the curb by the park.

"How long were you here yesterday?" Detective Evans asks.

"Almost two hours."

She gets out of the car and I follow, bringing my coffee with me. I reach back in to grab a piece of bacon. I want to feel better. If not better, at least different.

"A couple of uniforms have already been here and didn't see him," she says, putting her sunglasses on. "Is there anywhere he might hide?"

"I never let him out of my sight. I go wherever he goes. But he still likes to try and hide on me."

"Show me."

The park is immense. Three play structures, a soccer field, basketball courts, even a little skate park. All of this is bordered by trees and zigzagging trails.

We crawl around the play structure, calling Ben's name. There are plenty of places to hide here. I can remember hiding in them myself when I was a kid. My brother, Tom, and I spent hours here exploring the woods. Neither of us had a lot of friends back then. We just clung to one another. Especially after the divorce.

"Benny!" I yell. "Come out, come out, wherever you are."

The coffee is not sitting well. It's sloshing around in my stomach and thickening with the soggy sandwich and bacon. My brain feels as if it has been dropped into a carbonated drink.

"What about the woods?" Detective Evans asks.

"We go back there sometimes," I say, happy for the opportunity to not be crawling around in the sand. "The neighborhood kids build forts by the creek."

We take a well-worn path through the trees. At the bottom of the ravine, next to the creek, there are three forts made from broken branches, bits of plywood and old blankets and tarps. There's a massive tree beside them with boards nailed into its trunk. I climbed to the lowest branch with Benny a week ago. Once we made it there and settled comfortably on the branch, he got freaked out and wanted back down.

Detective Evans pulls a tarp from one of the rickety structures, and something scoots into the undergrowth. I lift the tarp roof from the next one and come nose to nose with a grisly, dirty face. I scream and jump back as a man emerges with a battered sleeping bag wrapped around his shoulders. He's coughing into his arm but keeping his eyes on me.

"Morning," Detective Evans calls, quickly covering the distance to stand in front of me. The man nods. "You been here all night?"

He coughs a couple more times and says, "Maybe."

"We're looking for a kid. A little boy." She takes a step forward and removes the tarp from the entrance to the fort. Detective Evans has a photo of Ben on her cell phone, and she holds it up in front of the man. "Seen him?"

As he squints at the screen, I look inside the fort. There are a couple of empty bottles and an empty KFC bucket.

"Nope," he says, eyeing Detective Evans's coffee.

"Would you like this? I've only had a sip or two."

The man reaches out and takes the cup. He puts it to his lips and closes his eyes. He smiles as he brings the cup away. "I love that feeling of the burning coffee on the lips and tongue. Makes you feel alive."

"It does," Detective Evans says.

Every time the man moves, I get a fresh waft of his odor.

"Do you stay here often?" Detective Evans asks.

"It's the suburbs, lady. People don't like people in the suburbs."

"Why are you here now?"

"Took the wrong bus," the guy says. He laughs, the effort turning into another coughing fit.

"But you've been here before?"

"Sure. It's peaceful. Sometimes it's nice to get away from the crowds, you know. I only come once it's dark, and I don't bother no kids. I'm usually gone by first light."

Detective Evans looks through the canopy at the sun. "Bit late, then, isn't it?"

"Church day," he says. "All the little ones 'round here are good Christians." He looks at me, probably trying to figure out what my role is in all of this.

"Listen, you should go to the shelter downtown," Detective Evans says. "It's a better place to stay. A nice bed rather than the cold ground."

"They kicked me out of the shelter last month for no goddamn reason."

"Here." She pulls a card and pen from her breast pocket, writes something on the back and hands the card to the man. "Take this to Peter, who runs the shelter. He knows me. Behave yourself and you'll have a good place to stay."

"Huh," the guy says with absolutely no feeling. "A cop."

"And I'd suggest you clear out of here before any kids are around. Right? You'd have the whole neighborhood up in arms if someone found you sleeping down here. You know how it is."

"I'm not hurting no one."

"I know it. But still." Detective Evans turns to me and puts a hand on my elbow. "See anything?"

The guy looks at me, waiting. I shake my head no.

"Okay. Let's head back." She gives the man a nod, and we clamber up the hill.

Some kids are on their way to the play structure, screaming and waving their arms, with their zombie parents trailing behind. There's a rustle of activity from the parents as they watch us clear the rise of the hill.

"That scare you?" Detective Evans asks once we're out in the sunlight.

"Not really," I lie. My heart is pounding. At least the jolt of adrenaline has momentarily lessened the headache.

"It'd be good if we could tag these kids," Detective Evans says as we cross the sand of the playground. The little kids have made it to the structure and are swinging and climbing as all kids do. A great mess of motion on the metal bars and plastic slides. The parents watch us as we close in on the cruiser.

"Tag?" I say.

"Yeah, like we do dogs and cats. Put a GPS in them. Then a kid goes missing, no worries—there's an app for that. Find him with your phone."

I don't respond. I can sense Detective Evans waiting for me to say something.

"I know," she says. "*Nineteen Eighty-Four*. Big Brother. Government spying. Privacy rights and all that. But if Benjamin had been tagged? We wouldn't be out here right now."

FOUR

Back in the cruiser, Detective Evans calls someone and berates them for their less-than-thorough search of the playground.

"A homeless guy came out of one of the kids' forts, Sean," she says. She listens for a moment while I wish I could put the window down. The engine is off, and with all the windows up, the heat is becoming unbearable. "Someone needs to talk to them. I don't care if it was the end of their shift. The mayor's son is missing. They obviously didn't do their job. How are we to know if they even got out of the cruiser?" There's a pause before she says, "Fine. Yes," and drops the phone into the cup holder where her coffee had been.

She starts the engine. "Where to now?"

Both windows descend, and blissfully cool air blows onto my skin. "The Dairy Queen."

"Which one?"

"Strondmount," I say.

"You went straight from there to here?" she asks.

"We finished our cones on the picnic table there."

She puts the windows back up and shuts the engine down.

"Let's walk it," she says. We watch as the homeless guy comes out of the woods. The zombie parents all sipping coffee from giant insulated mugs pretend he isn't there as he limps across the fresh grass to the road.

"What about before that?" Detective Evans asks.

"We were at the toy store down on Main. I forget the name of it."

"Loose Marbles," she says.

"Yeah, that's it."

"Don't sound so surprised. I know kids. I have two of my own. They go to Leslie Public School, just like I did." She gets out of the cruiser.

I set my phone down on the seat and gather up what's left of the breakfast sandwich and coffee. I have to shuffle the sandwich and the coffee around in order to open the door. As I slip out of the car, my stomach gives me another jolt.

"Did you take the path or the sidewalk?"

"The path," I say, shutting the car door and burping into a fist. "How old are your kids?"

"Twelve and ten. A boy and a girl."

"They at home?"

"At home with their dad. He pulls solo weekend duty when something like this happens."

I sip my coffee, wondering which way this walk is going to push my insides now that the day is becoming warmer. I've found that sometimes the fresh air calms my stomach down but other times gets everything rumbling and angry.

She points to the fork in the trail. "Left or right?"

"Left," I say. The right trail cuts close to the street. The left goes through the woods. Benny and I always go through the woods. My stomach heaves. The headache is rearing up again. I'm getting the pasties as well. I close my eyes for a moment against the sun and push at my glasses.

"How long does this walk normally take?" Detective Evans asks.

"From the Dairy Queen?" I try to think, but my brain is not functioning as it should. "Maybe fifteen minutes? Ben likes to go into the woods, then come back out and try to scare me."

"Fifteen. Okay. What is it, maybe eight, ten minutes otherwise?"

"I guess."

"Anywhere along here he could be hiding? The backyard of a house? Maybe down near the ravine?"

"No, it's nothing but forest back there. Honestly, Ben's a little afraid of the woods when it comes right down to it."

Detective Evans pulls out a pack of gum and offers me a piece.

"Thanks," I say. Chewing often calms me down. It might even settle my stomach a bit.

"So tell me, what is Benjamin's favorite thing in the world?" Detective Evans asks as she cuts over to a garbage can and drops the empty wrappers in.

I don't even have to think about it. "His mother."

It's a magical connection. They light up when they see one another. I see other kids at the playground disrespecting their parents. Yelling at them, demanding things and getting angry. But that never happens with Ben and Erin. They disagree now and then, but Ben takes it almost like an adult.

You can reason with him.

Take yesterday. Erin had just come from volunteering. Her father died when she was young, and she has no siblings, so when her mom died she was left entirely alone, in the sense that no one else understood the world she grew up in. So as much as she enjoys volunteering, feeling close to her mother again, it also leaves her tired and sad.

But still, when she came across the park and saw Ben, she lit up. It was as if the rest of the day had simply washed away.

"Really?" Detective Evans says. "His mom?"

"Yeah. He's a kid, so he's into games and toys and all that. He loves Star Wars and pretends to battle things with imaginary light sabers. But there's nothing he loves more than his mother."

"Really?" Detective Evans says again.

"Really."

"My kids..." she says, trailing off. "Paul is great in his way. Emma is..." She stops speaking, and we walk in silence until we reach the Dairy Queen, which, since it's Sunday morning, is closed. We go around to the back, and Detective Evans moves some boxes from beside a Dumpster.

Stale cones.

Moldy buns.

Empty drink containers.

No Ben.

But the smell! "You don't really think he'd be here, do you?" I say, staring at the garbage and trying not to breathe.

"We have to check everywhere," Detective Evans says. "You'd be surprised where we've found kids." She brushes her hands together. "Where were you before this?"

I back away from the stench in search of fresh air. "On the playground at the junior school."

"And before that?"

"Like I said, that Loose Marbles place."

Detective Evans looks at her phone again, swipes the screen, then puts it away. "Can you think of anywhere he might have gone? Not just from yesterday, but from any of the other days you've been with him. Some place he's talked about?"

"No, this is our route. Sometimes we go to a movie, but the rest of the time it's this park, the Dairy Queen, the toy store and the school."

Detective Evans looks around as if she might spot Ben sitting on a bench or strolling down the street.

"How do these things normally turn out?" I ask.

She doesn't stop to think. "You have three options. One, the kid ran off. There's usually a good reason for that. And some warning. And most likely he or she'll come back on his or her own. But five is pretty young for running away. And from what you're telling me, Benjamin isn't the most independent of kids. Plus, with him and his mom being like they are? I don't see it. Two, one of the parents has taken the kid. There's some kind of abuse going on in the home, or you're looking at a divorce and one of the parents feels like they'll lose the child, so away they go. But I don't see that either. Do you?"

"What?" I say. I'm trying to put as much distance between myself and the stink of garbage as possible.

"Have you seen abuse or anything with Benjamin?"

"From Jack?"

"Or Erin."

"No. Not at all. They're like…" I stare at the ground. "They're *perfect*."

"No family is perfect."

"They seem as close as you can get," I say.

"Well, they're both sitting home worried sick. When a parent takes a kid, they're gone in the middle of the night. Not at home calling the police."

"What's the third option?"

Detective Evans wrinkles her nose as she puts her sunglasses on. "Abduction. Someone watching the kid who decides, for whatever reason, to take him." I can see myself in her sunglasses when she turns toward me. "Benjamin's room is on the ground floor," she says.

"You don't think that's what happened," I say.

"We can't discount it. The window doesn't appear to be damaged. But the Carters' house doesn't have screens. Benjamin's window just had to be unlocked and someone could step right in."

"That can't be. There has to be a fourth option."

"If so, I don't know what it is," she says, beginning to walk again.

"There has to be something," I say.

"Such as?" Detective Evans says.

"He's hiding in a closet."

"Checked. The house has been swept."

"The attic?"

"We went through every inch."

"The tree house they have out back? It's totally enclosed. We play there sometimes." I can picture the tree house with its little fake shutters and Ben inside, eating Oreos until he's sick.

"It and the surrounding area as well. A canine unit is there now."

I imagine Benjamin being led by the hand across his moonlit lawn by some creep.

"Have you noticed anyone around?" Detective Evans asks.

"No," I say. Though I wouldn't necessarily know. Ben brings you into his own little world, and everything else disappears.

"Watching him from afar maybe? At the park or the Dairy Queen."

We've reached the school. The shaded windows are like mirrors. "I can't think of anyone anywhere," I say. "I honestly can't. It always seems to be the same people in the same places, you know?"

"Maybe you were sitting on a bench and he was playing? Someone came and talked to him?"

"I don't do that." I shake my head. "We always play together. Hide-and-seek or tag or Sandman."

"No one else is ever with you while you're babysitting?" Detective Evans asks, looking in a window.

"I used to go to this school," I say.

"Shouldn't Benjamin be in school? Mine started school when they were five."

"Erin wanted him home for the extra year. He'll go straight into first grade. A lot of kids do that. Did Erin mention anyone suspicious? Or maybe JJ or Steph have seen something?"

Detective Evans looks away from the window. She leans against the wall and looks out at the baseball diamond. "What I hear from Jack and Erin is that JJ and Stephanie aren't around their place much. Maybe every couple of weekends? Jack says it's because they're teenagers and have their own lives."

"Yeah?" I say, going up on tiptoes to look down the dark interior hallway. There's a wash of memories here. My old friends. The teachers. The ridiculousness of being herded into such a place five days a week. The single most important lesson is how to make teachers happy with the right attitude. Looking back, it seems absurd. There is no right attitude.

"What do you think?"

"About what?" I say. I look away from the window.

"Why JJ and Stephanie aren't around the Carter place much."

"I don't know. They live with their mom, right?"

"You ever see them over at the mayor's place?" Detective Evans asks.

"Sometimes. You don't think they have anything to do with Ben's disappearance, do you?"

"I'm trying to understand the family, that's all. Did you get a feel for how they are with Benjamin?"

"No. They talk with him, and Steph calls him cute, but that's about it. I saw JJ throwing a football with him one day, but football's not really Ben's thing."

"What do *you* think of them?"

"I don't know," I say, because I don't feel like getting into it with Detective Evans. Then she takes her sunglasses off and examines me, and I feel like I've been placed on the stand again.

"Everyone knows everyone in high school," she says. "What kind of reputation do they have?"

"JJ plays water polo and basketball," I say. "He works out a lot. Steph is…Steph spends a lot of time making certain she looks perfect. I don't mean that in a really negative way. She's a year younger than me and super popular."

"What about their friends?"

"I don't know," I say again. "Our school is weird. People go in their own groups, which pretty much leave one another alone. There's none of that jocks-beating-up-on-nerds stuff."

"JJ's in your grade, right? Do you two run in the same circles?" Detective Evans says.

Conversations with her are like building blocks. She has the end result in mind but needs to lead you there first. "Sometimes," I say. "But only if there's a larger group around. It's never a one-on-one thing. We're in the same History class, and earlier in the semester we did a group presentation together."

"Okay," she says. She sounds disappointed. I'm not certain where it was she wanted to lead me.

We stop at the end of the asphalt. The yard has a gentle slope to the playground and some tennis courts farther along. The rest of the view is residential. Duplexes, single-family homes, a block of row houses.

"So, where now?" I say.

Detective Evans is about to respond when a patrol car pulls into the parking lot and everything changes.

FIVE

A quick glance at her cell-phone screen, a slightly raised eyebrow, then, "I'll be right back." Detective Evans crosses the lawn to the opened window of the cruiser. I can't see who she's speaking with. Eventually she points toward the park, and the cruiser pulls away.

"Where's your brother?" Detective Evans asks as she nears me.

"Tom?"

"Yes," she says. "Where is Tom?"

"At home, I guess. Why?"

She holds her phone before her. "Call him."

"What's going on?"

"We need to know where he is."

"He doesn't have a cell," I say. "Why do you need to know where he is?"

"Call your house." Her sunglasses come off, revealing her penetrating stare. As if she's trying to read my mind. I open my mouth but am cut off before I can speak. "Call. Then I'll explain."

My mom answers on the first ring.

"Is Tom there?"

"Lauren?" A hazy, sleepy voice. It had seemed as though she was about to be hit by a migraine before I left the house. Everything she did was slow and delicate.

"Are you okay, Mom?"

"I was just about to lie down," she says.

"Mom, is Tom there?"

"I don't think so."

"Can you check his room?" I hear her moving through the house, then knocking on Tom's door, calling his name.

"He's not here."

"Okay," I say. I shake my head no at Detective Evans.

"Why are you looking for Tom? What's going on?" my mother asks.

"Tell your mom to sit tight," Detective Evans says. "We'll be right there."

"We'll be right back, Mom," I say.

"What's going on?" she asks. "What does Tom have to do with anything?"

"I don't know. We'll be right there." I hang up and hand the phone to Detective Evans.

She starts right back in on me. "Did Tom ever babysit Benjamin with you?" She's texting someone as she speaks.

"No," I say, then, "Well, not really. Sometimes he'd walk with us to the park or have ice cream. But he was never, like, officially there."

"Where does your brother hang out? Who are his friends?"

I stop.

Detective Evans takes another couple of steps, then turns back.

"What is going on?" I ask.

She pockets the phone. "Maybe nothing, Lauren."

"Then why all the questions about Tom?"

She puts her sunglasses back on so I can see myself again. "He was seen in the vicinity of the Carters' house last night."

"We do only live two blocks away."

"It's more than that, Lauren. A neighbor saw him out in front of the Carters' house around midnight."

"He could've been walking home," I say.

"He was across the street for more than twenty minutes. When the neighbor approached, your brother took off."

"How can you be sure it was Tom?"

"The man took a picture with his cell phone. He just now showed the photo to Erin and Jack, and they identified Tom."

"But you said that Tom took off, right?"

"He did. But we don't know where he went afterward."

"He probably came home," I say.

"Did you see him last night?" she asks.

I think of the hallway in my house and try to remember what it looked like when I stumbled in. Was Tom's door open or closed? Were his shoes on the mat? I can't remember. I don't even know how I got home.

"Maybe," I say.

"Let's go to your place and take a look, okay?"

And suddenly I have a hand on my back, pushing me forward. "What are you even saying? What could Tom possibly have to do with any of this? You can't think Tom *took* Ben. Can you?"

Her cell rings, and the hand disappears from my back. "Okay," she says. "I'm en route to the suspect's house. Can we keep the police presence down for the time being?" Listens again. "Thanks. Yes, I'll report in as soon as we're there." She pockets her phone as we pass the Dairy Queen.

"Suspect?" I say. "Do you mean Tom?"

"Have you ever heard of the seventy-two-hour rule, Lauren?"

"What?" I say. My head is pounding. My skin feels moist and electric. I'm getting really tired of the way Detective Evans feels the need to end all her sentences with *Lauren*.

"If a missing child isn't found within seventy-two hours, the likelihood he or she ever will be drops dramatically."

"You said *suspect*," I say. "You were talking about my brother and you used the word *suspect*."

"I did."

We move quickly and silently. I have a million questions I want to ask her, but I feel so ill and dazed that I simply follow along.

— — — —

"Tell me about your brother," Detective Evans says as I slam the car door shut. She's reading something on the in-car computer.

"He would never hurt anyone."

"Okay. But what is he like?"

My coffee has gone cold. The car smells of grease and sweat. When I got in, I had to grab my cell phone off the seat before sitting down. "He's a guy," I say.

"He's a grade ahead of you, right? But he goes to Mitchell Mayer High?"

"He was living with my dad downtown for a while. When my dad moved to California, Tom decided to keep going there. He'll graduate this year."

"So he's eighteen?"

"Seventeen. His birthday is Thursday. For one week a year we're the same age. Like, the same number age." I've always found this interesting, but it sounds really stupid when I actually say it.

Detective Evans presses the touchpad on the computer, and her eyes dance from side to side as she reads. "He's a big guy." She looks at me.

"Kind of."

"But you're…well, you're not, and your mother isn't…"

"And my dad isn't fat either. Back in grade school, when my parents were going through their divorce and everything, Tom started eating. Like, whenever he was upset or worried, he'd eat."

"Divorce is tough on kids." Detective Evans starts the car and backs out of the parking lot.

I press the button to lower the window but nothing happens. My hangover has shifted into high gear, and I'm overheating and shaky and would rather be curled up in bed feeling sorry for myself.

"Do you two get along?" she asks.

"We don't have a lot of the same friends or anything, if that's what you mean."

"So you don't spend much time together?"

"Pretty much none."

"Who are his friends?"

"I don't know," I say. Which sounds better than *He doesn't have any.*

"What *can* you tell me, Lauren?"

"Like I said before, the divorce was really tough on Tom. Our dad decided that Tom should live with him. Tom agreed to go, I think only because he didn't want it to be a giant battle. We saw what the divorce was doing to our mom, and I guess Tom figured he could save her from the worst of it if he just went. So we'd still see one another on weekends, but it started getting awkward right away. Like, he started changing. Closing in on himself." I look at her. "But none of that matters. I know he would never do anything to Benny."

"So he knows Benjamin?" Detective Evans says.

"I already told you he does."

"When was the last time he saw Benjamin?"

We're almost at my house, stopped at a crosswalk where once, long ago, I'd stepped into the street in front of a car and Tom had pulled me back at the last second. The streets are stained with a million of these memories.

"Yesterday," I admit. "He saw Ben yesterday."

SIX

"I was in bed early," Mom says. The living room is settled in darkness. I go about opening the curtains as she speaks. "I had to take something for my migraine, and it knocked me right out."

Detective Evans has already pawed through Tom's room. "He doesn't have a computer?"

"He's never wanted one," Mom replies.

"No cell phone either, I understand. That's a bit different for a kid his age."

"Tom has never gone in for electronics. I don't know what to say." She wrings her hands. "He's only been living here for half a year."

I crank open a window. "Mom," I say, "I'll talk to Detective Evans about Tom, okay?"

"He moved in with his father all those years ago and…" She covers her face.

I want to tell her it was Tom's choice. A decision had to be made. Sure, it was an easy out for everyone, but no one knew at the time that it would be so hard on Tom.

Detective Evans is leveling that penetrating stare at my mother now. A new target. A new file to draw information from. "And that was a difficult situation?"

Mom nods to this. "Maybe we should have tried to work things out," she offers.

"That's not always the best plan."

"No, you're right. Things could have been worse," Mom says.

"Sometimes it helps to simply see our kids as people," Detective Evans says. "Everyone has a flaw or two."

"That is certainly true," Mom says.

"But do you believe he could have taken this child?" Detective Evans says.

"No. Absolutely not. Tom has had his difficulties, but he…No." She's holding her head as though it might explode.

"Mom," I say. "Go lie down, okay? I'll talk with Detective Evans." I help her to her bed, close the curtains and turn off the light.

"It'll be okay, Mom," I say before leaving the room.

———

"How do we find him, Lauren?" Detective Evans asks when I return.

"I told you before, I don't know," I say.

Detective Evans looks at her phone. "Could you turn the TV on to channel four?"

"Why?" I say, already looking for the remote.

"There's something you should see."

I turn the TV on to find pictures of Ben and Tom on the screen. "What is this all about?" I say.

"Watch."

"If you have any information regarding the whereabouts of Benjamin Dale Carter or Thomas Evan Saunders," the announcer says, "please call the local authorities. Both are missing and may possibly be traveling together."

I stare at the pictures. Ben's photo is one I took at the park a week ago. Tom's is his yearbook photo. I start to speak, but Detective Evans interrupts me.

"We're not saying Tom has anything to do with Benjamin's disappearance, Lauren. Just that we would like to talk with him." She sits on the couch and flips the TV remote from one hand to the other, back and forth, watching me. "It's the best I could do under the circumstances."

"Why?" I say. "Because he was walking in our neighborhood last night and someone got freaked out? This is insane."

"You know why we need to speak with him, Lauren."

I look at the picture of Tom again before it disappears. It seems as though it's been cropped from the yearbook. I wonder how they managed to get it so quickly.

"I don't think I want to talk to you anymore," I say. "Please just go." The Amber Alert has disappeared and been replaced by a talk show.

"You could help us find him, Lauren."

"Find who? Ben or my brother?"

"Lauren. You *must* know some of the places he goes. The people he connects with. We just need one lead. Someplace to start."

"I don't know anything," I say. "Please go."

"Lauren," Detective Evans says, "JJ told us about that day in the park."

"That was a total misunderstanding," I say.

"Nevertheless, it is causing us some concern."

"It shouldn't. Nothing happened."

"Lauren—" she begins, but I've had enough.

"Go!"

"Lauren, I need you to try to help your brother here. I need—"

"I need you to go," I say, and I must look crazy because Detective Evans pulls a card from her pocket and lays it on the coffee table, then backs away.

"I'll go. It's okay, Lauren. I know this is difficult. But if he comes back here, you need to call me. Do you understand? I can't say what will happen if someone else finds him first." Her cell rings as she's opening the door to leave. She answers it, there on the threshold. Looks back at me.

"It's Erin," she says, holding the phone out and switching it to speaker.

"Lauren?" Erin's voice fills the room. "Lauren, can you hear me?"

"Yes," I say.

"Lauren, would you mind coming over here with Detective Evans?"

I stare at the stupid green carpet. I've hated this carpet since day one. So did my dad. It was one of the last things he mentioned before walking out the door. This stupid green carpet.

What a mess.

"Lauren," Erin says. "Please."

"Okay," I say. "Fine."

SEVEN

The Carters.

Erin, Jack, JJ and Steph.

They're all here.

We enter through the kitchen, avoiding most of the madness. There are news vans and journalists outside. A group of them moved toward the cruiser as we pulled in. A uniformed officer had to shield us, arms out, shaking his head as photographs were taken. I wonder if this much attention would be given to Benny if his father wasn't the mayor.

I spot JJ standing beside a fit-looking female officer, a few strands of his perfectly coiffed hair gently waving in the air-conditioned breeze. The officer stifles a laugh at something JJ says, and he straightens up.

Steph is at the kitchen table, a book of photographs in front of her. She immediately stands when she spots Detective Evans. "I don't recognize anyone in here," she says. I catch her glance. The one she saves for the unworthy.

"I'd like you to keep going, Stephanie," Detective Evans tells her.

"I'm never with Ben," she says.

"But you might have noticed one of these men nearby. Maybe at a park or outside your house. Maybe not even when you were with Benjamin."

"They're all starting to look the same," she whines.

"Stephanie, you told us you wanted to help in any way you could. This is helping."

"I don't notice old guys, and these guys are all old *and* creepy."

"Please, Stephanie," Detective Evans says.

Steph closes her eyes and exhales sharply. "I need to make a smoothie before I can go on," she says, opening the fridge. She's wearing a pair of shorts only slightly larger than the panties beneath. A blue dress shirt is open farther down than it should be and tied above her waist.

"Thank you," Detective Evans says. She moves me through the kitchen toward the living room. We're no more than three steps in before I find myself wrapped in Erin's arms.

"We're going to find him," she says. Her eyes are huge, round, red-rimmed. She nods in agreement with herself. "We are." She releases me. Erin is thin and has these perfectly formed lips. Her hair is tied up now, but when it's down it's a great, flowing waterfall of curls. She has big green eyes, just like Benny. Strangely, for a woman her age, she's never had her ears pierced. In fact, she rarely wears any jewelry at all. There have been a few times at the park when people asked if we're sisters. Though I think that's more about how young Erin looks than because of any similarities we might possess.

"Let's go outside," Detective Evans says. "Where it's a little quieter."

As we're stepping out the patio doors, Jack Carter is coming toward us, cell phone pressed to his ear. He stops to let us out, covering the phone with one hand.

"Who's this?" he asks, gesturing at me.

"This is Lauren Saunders, Jack," Erin says. "You know Lauren—she looks after Benny."

He looks at me in the way people look at foreign fruit.

"Of course," he says. I can tell he doesn't recognize me at all. "Yes, yes, of course." He reaches out and pats me on the shoulder, then puts the phone to his ear again as he goes inside and closes the patio door behind him with a bang.

The pool glows in the early-afternoon burn of the sun. We sit at a glass table on well-cushioned chairs.

"Can you think of anywhere he might be?" Erin asks. And I know that she, unlike Detective Evans, means Ben, not Tom.

"No. I'm sorry—I just can't," I say.

"Lauren has been with me all morning," Detective Evans says. "She has been very helpful."

"What about your brother?" Erin says, never taking her eyes off me. "I saw his picture on the TV...but he couldn't have done this."

"No," I say. "He couldn't have."

"No, of course not," Erin agrees. "He's your brother."

I have my cell out, rubbing its side and staring at the blank screen.

"It's like we've raised him together," Erin says, turning to Detective Evans. "Ben looks up to Lauren. She's always taken very good care of him. I never worry about him when he's with her."

"Have you thought of anywhere he might be? Anywhere at all?" Detective Evans says. Her tone has changed. It's lighter, though she could just be playing good cop with Erin.

"No," Erin says. "I have been racking my brain, and no. He's always either with me or with Lauren."

"You've had some time now, Erin. Can you recall seeing anyone around? A stranger you may have noticed on more than one occasion?"

Erin shakes her head. "No. I've tried and tried. I did what you said and walked through my days in my mind. But I can't think of anyone. I didn't notice anyone watching us, I mean. Maybe I'm not observant enough."

"What about you, Lauren? Have you thought of anyone who might have been watching you?" Detective Evans asks.

She seems to have forgotten about me yelling at her to get out of my house. It's like her ability to shift into a completely different person somehow allows her to pretend nothing has happened.

"No," I say. "No one."

She turns back to Erin. "We're examining some of the closed-circuit camera footage at the stores you've visited recently. We'll be looking to see if the same face pops up more than once. If we find anyone, we'll have you look at the footage right away."

"Okay," Erin says, nodding.

I can only imagine what a parent in this type of situation must go through. Every ounce of new information must feel like a glimmer of hope.

"We're going to find him, Erin. I know we will," Detective Evans says. She reaches out and puts a hand on Erin's shoulder.

Erin swallows and nods again. "The thought of someone taking him. The things that could—"

"Don't think like that, Erin. It's not good."

"Oh God, some little room or a basement and…"

"Erin," Detective Evans says. "You can't…"

I sense something in my peripheral vision and look up to find JJ at the patio door. He's just standing there, staring out at me. He has his cell phone in one hand and a Coke Zero in the other. His expression doesn't change when I look at him. He keeps staring as though somehow I can't see him, like the glass door is a one-way mirror and he could stand there watching me forever and I'd never be the wiser.

He suddenly looks over his shoulder, then moves to the side as a male officer opens the patio door and steps out.

"Detective, we've found something on the closed circuit from the grocery store."

"What is it?" Detective Evans says.

The officer has these ridiculously blue eyes. A really deep blue. I stare at them, which is, I assume, why he glances at me before he speaks.

"Tom Saunders, Detective."

— — — —

The video is black and white and grainy. It's washed in stuttered motions. It isn't truly video, the officer explains. It's a still camera taking thousands of snapshots a day, then splicing them together.

The officer points at Erin and Ben on the laptop screen. "This was last Wednesday at the Whole Foods."

Ben is in the shopping cart's seat. He has his favorite stuffed animal, a elephant, clutched in his little hands. Erin seems to be examining her receipt.

"And if we advance a few frames..." the officer says, moving the pictures along. "Yes, right here. This is Tom Saunders, correct?"

It is.

It's Tom.

It's really difficult to miss him. He's standing at the end of an aisle at the front of the store. The officer advances a few more frames. It's hard to tell because of the quality of the picture, but it looks like Tom is watching Ben and Erin as they pass. At the last second, as Erin and Ben are leaving the area, Tom raises a hand and waves.

"He leaves a second later," the officer says.

"Did you speak to Tom that day, Erin?" Detective Evans asks.

"No. I had no idea he was there." She looks at me as if I might be able to decipher what we are seeing.

"Benjamin didn't say anything?" Detective Evans says.

"Nothing. I remember looking at my receipt. There was something on it that I wasn't certain I'd meant to buy. So I was in my own little world. We left the store and came straight back here."

"Moving on to the next day," the officer begins, cueing something on the computer.

Erin interrupts him. "The next day I went back because we needed cream cheese. That was what it was. I'd picked up cottage cheese rather than cream cheese by mistake."

"Yes, we have that here as well." He advances a new recording. The grainy picture shifts slowly along. Everyone looks like out-of-sync zombies. "Here you are at the customer-service counter. If we wait a moment, we'll see Tom Saunders."

"He was there again?" Erin says.

I turn around to find JJ across the room, arms crossed, staring at me. Or at the video screen. I can't tell. But when I look at him, he again doesn't look away.

"He was. He came in less than a minute after you." Tom moves into the store, looks around, then enters an aisle where he has a clear view of Ben in the cart. Erin finishes paying for the cream cheese, all the while holding Ben's hand. As they're about to leave, Erin stops to talk to someone.

"That's Katherine Hobbs, the councilor," Erin says.

"Yes," the officer says. "Someone is contacting her now."

"Why?" Erin asks.

"Just wait." In the video, Ben twists from side to side on the link of his mother's arm. The two women go on talking. At the end of the aisle, Tom stands stock-still, watching. He waves and Ben waves back.

"So they know one another," the officer says. Everyone looks at me.

"Yes, I told you that already," I say. "Tom would sometimes come to the park with us."

"But the interesting thing is that Benjamin doesn't let his mother know Tom is there. And if you look here," the officer says, leaning forward, "it seems as if Tom has raised a finger to his lips. And Ben nods in return."

Everyone looks at me again, as if I can explain any of this.

"Are you entirely certain you have no idea where your brother is?" Detective Evans says.

I inhale quickly, trying to keep my emotions in check. "I honestly don't," I say. I'm about to go on. To tell them how Tom and I grew apart when he moved in with our dad, and we've only recently begun to talk again about anything of any importance. I say, "I wish I could help, but I can't."

"I know, Lauren," Erin says. "I know."

JJ's voice comes loud and sharp from behind us. "That freak took my brother!"

"JJ," Erin says.

"He's always been like this. There was that kid in the park." JJ is right beside me now, his finger in my face. "Where'd he take Ben?"

"He wouldn't—"

"He did it before."

I close my eyes. When I open them, I find Steph watching me. She gives a quick headshake and narrows her eyes.

"JJ," Detective Evans begins.

"We found him bugging this kid in the park. This was three years ago," JJ says. Everyone has fallen silent. "The kid said Tom was trying to get him to go into the woods with him."

"He was asking what the boy was building," I say. "The kid was playing in the sand, and Tom asked him—"

"Bullshit. He's a creep and he's finally grabbed a kid. We all knew it would happen." JJ turns to Detective Evans. "It's like I told you. We chased him, but he got away. If we'd caught him that day we would have—"

"Okay, JJ." Jack Carter's voice booms over the crowd. Everyone turns to find him standing at the door to the kitchen. "That's enough."

"Her creepy brother took him, Dad."

"JJ," the mayor says again. "Enough."

"Where does he go? Huh? Who does he hang out with? We find Tom, we find Ben." JJ is too close to me, but there's nowhere for me to move. For some reason, no one immediately steps between JJ and me. Detective Evans is within arm's reach, but she just stands there, watching.

Erin finally stands and slips in between us. "JJ, this isn't helping anything. We're doing all we can here."

"All we need to do is find her freak brother," JJ says. He backs away from his stepmother, then pushes through the crowd of people and is gone. Steph lingers, her phone out in front of her. She's texting someone. She looks up at me one last time before turning and following her brother down the hall.

EIGHT

Erin catches me trying to sneak out of the house while no one is looking. She doesn't say anything. She just holds my shoulders for a moment before I leave.

I cut across the neighbor's lawn in order to dodge the journalists outside. The crowd has expanded to include talking heads doing stories with the Carter house as a backdrop.

I don't expect to find the same thing at my house, but as I approach, I see six journalists standing around drinking coffee and chatting with one another. One of them, a redhead in a pantsuit, recognizes me and rushes down the sidewalk to intercept me.

"Lauren Saunders?" she says. I duck my head down and try to pass by her, but she steps in front of me. "Just a couple of questions, Lauren, please."

"I don't have anything to say," I manage.

"Do you know where your brother, Tom Saunders, is?" She thrusts a microphone into my face.

"No. I have no idea," I say.

"Can you explain why he would have done something like this?"

I stop.

"He didn't," I say.

"So you have spoken to him?"

"No."

"Then how can you be certain he has nothing to do with the disappearance of Benjamin Carter?"

"Because he doesn't," I say. I try to push past her again.

"Can you tell us about this previous incident involving your brother and a young boy?"

"Nothing happened," I said. "It was a misunderstanding."

"Can you explain to us what this misunderstanding was, Lauren Saunders?"

"No," I finally say. Which is all I should have said in the first place. I push past her and run up the driveway with my head down.

My father's voice assaults me the second I step inside the door. "This is why he should have moved out here with me."

I look around for him, somehow thinking that he has actually returned to Resurrection Falls to see us. I am, inexplicably, hopeful for a moment.

You have to understand my father. He's used to getting what he wants. He once wanted my mother, and he got her. He wanted out of the marriage and managed that as well. He wanted Tom, and Tom went to live with him downtown. Though that's a little more difficult to understand. My father would never admit it, but it's pretty evident that he only ever wanted Tom in order to hurt my mother. Tom had always been her little boy. I won't say her favorite, because I can't see her truly having favorites. When she was ill, Tom would be there for her. He would pick up her medication. Make her soup. Bring her water and warm face cloths. Unlike our father, Tom thought of others first.

I think our father saw this and decided Tom needed to be a man. Needed to be more like him.

"I suppose," my mother says. I can see her now, on the couch, her cell phone propped up before her. My father's voice, filled with static, is coming through the little speaker. "But he's been doing so well here, and—"

"He's abducted a child, Janet."

I stand beside the couch and look at my mother. Her face is red and streaked with tears. I hold my hands out in a questioning manner.

"That doesn't sound all that well," my father says, mocking her tone.

"Oh, Michael, Lauren's here now. Maybe she has some—"

"What's going on, Lauren? What's your brother done?"

"Nothing," I say.

"I've been getting calls from the police and reporters. How did anyone get my number?"

"I guess it's listed?" I say.

"Did you give people my number?"

"No, Dad. Why would I—"

"Where is he, Lauren? You must know."

"I don't," I say. "I need to talk to Mom. We'll call if we hear anything." I grab my mother's phone.

"The second you hear from Tom, or they catch him, you call me."

"Fine," I say, hanging up.

My mother is staring into space. Shaking her head.

"Why were you talking to him?" I ask.

"He called."

"He always upsets you."

She inhales deeply. "He's your father," she says, as if this explains anything. As if he's actually been anything even close to a dad.

"He's useless and cruel," I say.

"Lauren, he's your *father*," she repeats.

"And that means I'm supposed to respect him?" I sit down beside her, and she leans her head on my shoulder. I've never been as good as Tom at comforting her. I sometimes fear that there's a bit of my father's cruelty in me. Or, at the very least, his disregard for others' feelings. I notice it sometimes as well. The way I have passed over friends without really caring.

Like last semester, when some of the girls at school were playing this stupid game. Steph Carter started it. She'd go up to some of the bigger girls and ask them how they slept at night: *You know, back, front, left, right? Which side do you sleep on?*

The girls were always confused by the question. First of all, who cares, right? And second, Steph Carter had likely never said a word to them before, so the sudden interest was confounding.

But for some reason, they would always answer. You watch something like this happen and you can see how people get pulled into cults, gangs, fundamentalist beliefs. These girls wanted to believe that Steph, super-popular Steph Carter, actually cared about them. Cared what they thought, what they did, how they slept at night.

If the girl said *right side*, there'd be an immense amount of hilarity because, apparently, pigs always sleep on their right side. The girl would find her way onto Steph's piggy list, which was distributed online for all to see.

My friend Stacy had done it once in a blatant grab at popularity. She asked this girl Marlene, but Marlene had already heard of the piggy test and refused to answer.

No answer means right side, piggy. On the piggy list you go, Stacy had said.

When we were little kids, Marlene and I played together all the time. We were absolutely best friends. Right up to about eighth grade, before we went off to high school and everything changed.

Why do you have to be like that? Marlene had asked. *Why do you have to be such a bitch all the time?*

Why do you have to be so fat and disgusting all the time? Stacy had replied before grabbing my hand and dragging me away.

I'd made the mistake of looking back. Marlene was watching us go. She was shaking her head, and I could tell she was sad. But not for herself. It really didn't look pitiful. It looked pitying.

Lesson: never look back.

"Don't talk to him anymore," I say to my mom.

"He needs to be kept informed." I notice the bucket beside the couch. These migraines are often so awful that she's left throwing up, dizzy and discombobulated.

"I'll take care of it," I say. "Do you want to be out here or in bed?"

"It doesn't matter," she says. Then she looks directly at me. "Do you think he could have done it?"

"Abducted Ben?" I say.

"Yes."

"No way," I say. "He would never snatch a kid. How can you even think that, Mom?"

"I worry," she says.

"What do you worry about?"

"That I never should have let him go."

The truth is, she shouldn't have. No one should have been forced to live with my father. But she didn't force him. She just let him go. It's almost the same, but not quite.

"He went," I say. "He did it for all of us. So there wasn't so much fighting. I don't think he could take the fighting any longer."

"I know he couldn't have done something like this. Not our Tom," Mom says. "I never thought he could. I hope I haven't damaged him."

"You didn't," I say. "He's the same old Tom."

"I think I'll go to bed," she says. "Wake me up if he comes home."

I help her to her feet, and she shuffles off to her bedroom. "I will, Mom," I say. Then, for the second time in the same day, I say, "It's going to be okay." As if I can promise something like that.

I step into my own very messy bedroom and slam the door. I look at my bed like the oasis it is. But before I give up on the day, I go to the bathroom. I felt gross when I woke up this morning, and nothing I have done during the day has changed this. I take a long hot shower, then look in the mirror.

Bad idea.

I look at my freckles and hate them.

My big nose. Hate that too.

My too-small breasts. Hate both of them equally.

My hair. Hate it. What possessed me to get bangs? They're too short. I look like Velma from *Scooby-Doo*.

I've been slowly attempting to reinvent myself. You can't do these things all at once or people notice, and they won't give you an inch. They'll mock you for trying. But for so long I was my brother's sister. The two of us were so close in age that we always hung out together. Then the divorce happened, and he moved across town and I was on my own. There had been a group of us kids in the neighborhood who all hung out together. But once we hit high school, everyone found new friends with similar interests. I mostly kept to myself.

The parties started in my sophomore year. I don't even know why I went to the first one. I guess it was because I had one friend left, Stacy, and she really, really wanted to go, to talk to some boy or other.

I'd never had more than a glass of wine before. But I was so bored at the party, and felt so out of place, that whenever someone would hand me a drink, I'd take it.

Then the shot glasses came out, and somehow I became the life of the party.

I heard someone say, *I didn't know she was so fun!*

I still have no idea who that was, but whoever it was changed me. I'd always been *Tom's sister*. Or *that girl with the bad hair and glasses*. After that party, I decided I wanted to be someone different. Someone fun. I bought contacts, dressed a bit nicer, worried about my makeup. And no one said a word. No one called me a fake or tried to knock me back down again. I was Lauren Saunders, the life of the party. I made new friends, though I never really felt close to any of them. But it seemed fine. It seemed like what people do.

I leave my glasses in the bathroom and turn away from the mirror.

I lie down on my bed and stare at the ceiling. My body sinks into the mattress. I can feel my muscles releasing. It's getting dim outside, but not dark enough for the journalists to depart. They're out there interviewing the neighbors.

I can already hear the sound bites:

"He seemed so normal."

"I wouldn't think he would be the type."

"They have had their troubles, certainly. The father moved away, you know. The mother is often ill."

A new story is being created out there. A new truth. A new identity for all of us.

I pull my duvet over me, even though it's warm in my room, and close my eyes. It will be okay, I tell myself. Everything is going to be all right.

NINE

I wake up just after ten feeling a lot better but incredibly hungry. My contacts are in their little jar beside the bed. I pop them in, open my bedroom door and look out. My mom will be asleep. She often sleeps for twelve or thirteen hours after taking her medication. She tells me that every day she wakes up and hopes things will be different. That her head will feel different. That she won't be bowled over by the migraines.

But every day is exactly the same.

I go to the kitchen and make a sandwich and pour a glass of orange juice. I sit on the couch and turn the TV on.

After some fascinating stories about pandas, a windstorm somewhere out west and bushfires in Australia, a picture of Ben appears.

A tall blond woman with brown eyes is discussing the situation with an anchorman. "The boy has now been missing for at least fourteen hours. Investigators cannot say exactly when he disappeared."

"So what do we know, Kim?" the anchorman asks.

"We know that Benjamin Carter, our mayor's son, disappeared sometime in the night. He was last seen wearing a Thomas the Tank Engine pajama set. That is, both top and bottoms."

"Are there any suspects, Kim?"

"Not at the moment, no. However, someone with inside knowledge of the case who wishes to remain anonymous told me the police are interested in locating one Thomas Saunders. My source tells me that he may not be directly involved in the child's abduction, but it is possible he has information the police could use at this desperate time."

"Is there anything else the public could do?"

"Well, currently Thomas Saunders's whereabouts are unknown. So if anyone out there sees Thomas or Benjamin, contact the authorities immediately." Tom's yearbook picture flashes on the screen. In it, he looks almost happy.

"Kim, have you had the opportunity to speak with the mayor?"

"Mayor Carter has asked that his privacy be respected."

"And, of course, it will be, Kim. Thank you. And let's hope this little boy returns soon. I know the authorities will be doing all they can." The anchorman opens his mouth to speak, but I shut the TV off before I have to hear another word. I stare at the blank screen while I finish my sandwich. Then I go into my room, put on a pair of jeans and a hoodie, remove the window screen and slip outside.

There is only a half-moon, but it's a cloudless night. The lawn is thick and nighttime green beneath my feet. The long blades tickle my ankles as I move toward the tree house.

When we were kids, Tom and I would sneak out of the house at night. This was after the divorce, while Tom was still living with us, and our parents were debating our fates with strangers in court. We'd go barefoot out on the cool, dark lawn. The moon high in the sky, the stars unbearably bright.

We never went far. In fact, we never left the confines of the backyard. The previous owners had built this tree house in the corner of the lot. It had four walls and a roof, and you had to climb up a ladder at the bottom.

We didn't really do anything. Most of the time we were silent, listening. Cars moving along the street behind us. Adults laughing. That slow rise and fall of voices and noise.

I climb the ladder and pull myself through. I can't recall the last time I was inside. It smells musty and damp.

A kiddie table-and-chair set left over from the previous owners dominates the space. Tom and I never moved them from their original spot. How long has it been since I've climbed in here? Eight, ten years?

It seems like a lifetime ago.

I lean against the wall and close my eyes. I can hear the crickets chirping away and cars passing by on the street. The smell brings back a hundred memories. Weeks used to go by where only Tom and I would play together. No friends. No one from the outside world. Just the two of us and our imaginations. This tree house has been a castle, a coffin, a luxurious seaside home, an ice-fishing hut.

We played cards in here: Uno, Hearts and Go Fish. Later, we had handheld video games. I push my feet out and can almost feel Tom's feet pushing back. That was how we would sit. Feet to feet.

But we grew too tall. So then we stretched out, backs against one wall, feet against the other. I try this and don't come close to fitting. I have to bend my knees and lean forward. I open my eyes and look out the tiny window at the moon. Tom would tell me stories about people living on the moon. Even then I knew they were made up, but I loved his stories.

Other times we would stay silent and listen to the night noises. Sometimes I would fall asleep, and Tom would eventually wake me and we'd go back inside. He would never leave me out here.

When the divorce was finalized, Tom suddenly lived at the other end of town and went to a different school, and we barely saw one another. My father was often too busy to see me on his weekends, and a few times I didn't see Tom for over a month. At first I didn't think much of it. I mean,

I missed him. But other than that, it didn't seem strange. My father was busy, so he couldn't bring Tom to see us. That was it.

Our mother never fought for it either. She was deep in the blinding world of migraines by then, and the thought of having to entertain two kids for a whole weekend must have been crippling.

Tom was mostly quiet when we saw one another. He'd ask about people at school and about how I was doing in different classes. Whenever I asked how he was, he'd shrug and say he was fine.

I let it go.

I let it drop.

I let him be completely alone.

I take a final look around the tree house, then climb down the ladder. I start toward my bedroom, but I'm too awake to go to sleep. If I go inside, I'll end up messing around on the Internet or watching more television. So instead, I turn around and slip through a hole in the hedge that runs the length of the backyard.

It's not so late that the world has stopped. Televisions flash blue and orange behind curtains. People are walking their dogs, plastic bags jammed in pockets. Headlights cut holes through the darkness.

I've walked three blocks when I get the strange feeling that someone is following me. I can't say where the feeling comes from, but one second I'm thinking how nice it is to be alone, and the next second it feels as though someone is right behind me, following my every step. I slow down as I pass a bus stop and quickly turn. I don't see anyone, though a car pulls to the curb a half block back, and the headlights flash off.

I begin walking again—slowly, waiting to hear the car doors open and close. Just as I'm starting to get freaked out, there are voices and laughter and doors slamming shut. I take another quick look back. There's no one near the car, and because of where it is parked, I can't tell if anyone is inside either.

I turn the corner onto Spruce Avenue and find myself across the street from the Carters' house. I can see the bench where Tom sat the night before. The driveway is filled with cars. The curtains are all drawn, but the house is awash with light.

Steph's little red Jetta—a gift from her father—is in the driveway. Steph and JJ live with their mother in a big house in a different part of town. JJ used to have a Ford Taurus, which looked completely ordinary on the outside but had been tricked out for street racing. It was stolen right out of his mother's driveway. From what I heard, whoever took it must have known a lot about alarm systems, because the only way to actually steal it without setting off sirens and having the engine lock down would've been to load it onto a flatbed and drive it ever so gently away.

I get up before anyone can notice my presence and round the next corner, figuring I'll do a quick block and go home. I stare at the ground as though I might be able to see

Tom's footsteps glowing on the ground. As if I can follow them and find him at the end, safe and sound.

I snap out of my daze and remember that this street is a cul-de-sac. I turn around to discover a guy walking toward me. He immediately changes direction and crosses the street.

I move as quickly as possible back to Spruce Avenue, which is, thankfully, well lit. I take a quick look in the direction the guy went but can't spot him.

When I turn the corner to the street behind my house, I start running and then jump through the hedge and into my yard. I sit there for a moment, trying to calm my breathing and watching to see if anyone was following me.

As I'm about to give up, a figure detaches itself from behind a tree across the street. Whoever it is crosses the road, takes a quick look toward where I am crouched behind the hedge, then walks away.

A moment later a cruiser passes and circles the block. As I cross the yard, I can see the cruiser moving slowly past the front of my house.

I climb back into my bedroom and replace the screen. I stand for a moment looking out on the dim lawn before closing the window and securing the lock.

I change into my pajamas, turn off the light and crawl beneath my covers. "It was a journalist," I say into the darkness. Someone out to get a story. Trying to break some big story of a child abduction. It had to be.

I inhale and wait for my heart to slow. The moon shines in my window. My family is under a microscope now. That's a fact. It's something I'm going to have to live with.

I close my eyes and try to sleep.

TEN
MONDAY

It's always difficult to pay attention to Mr. King's history lessons, but this morning it feels absolutely mission impossible. Almost everyone has a cell in his or her hands and is slightly hunched over, reading from the screen, while Mr. King endlessly writes things on the board.

I'm staring out the window to where kids are running track and throwing balls on the football field. For a brief moment it almost feels like a normal day.

Mr. King talks about a declaration that isn't the Independence one. I have no idea what this class is even about.

I turn around to find JJ Carter staring at me. By the angle of his body, it seems as though he may have been in this position since he arrived. His face doesn't change as I look at him. I have often felt invisible to JJ. So much so that now, when he finally sees me, it's as if he doesn't know how to pretend I exist. I'm still nothing but a thing in the world, but now I'm a thing he has to deal with.

I turn back around and do my best to pay attention to Mr. King. Honestly, though, it's been too long gone. I swear I'll pay more attention when he gets into whatever is next in this course. Soon enough, class ends. No one speaks to me as I gather up my books. I do get a lot of looks. Sideways looks, full-on stares, quick glances that settle and then scoot around the room.

The hallway is filled with people changing classes, opening and closing lockers and yelling ridiculous things at one another. A trail of whispers has been following me since I entered the school. A hush pulses out before me as I move through the hallway.

"There she is," JJ Carter says. I hadn't noticed him standing there in a pack of his friends, but soon he is beside me. "Where's your brother at?" he demands.

He's got himself all puffed up. I'm not sure how he managed to make the basketball team—he's slightly shorter than I am. "I don't know," I say.

"Bullshit. How can you not know?" JJ says.

"I haven't seen him in a couple of days."

"How's that possible? Don't you, like, live in the same house?"

"Sure, but—"

"So where is he?" JJ moves forward, and one of his friends, Ralph "Mac" Mackenzie, leans into him a bit.

"Dude, relax. She says she doesn't know, so she doesn't know. Let it drop." Mac's always been kind to me. Before he made the basketball team, he was like me: a tall, lanky outsider. Now he's a star point guard, and people look up to him in a different way.

"She has to know." JJ turns to me. "He'd better not've hurt Ben." His eyes are on fire, and his breath is awful. He's made a little gun of his fingers and is pointing it at me.

"Tom has nothing to do with it," I say.

"What makes you so sure? What was that creep doing outside my house? Huh?" A disgusted look overtakes his face. "If you were a dude, I'd beat the information out of you right here, right now."

"Guy," Mac says. "You have to chill out."

"I don't have to do anything," JJ says, pushing Mac aside. "I swear to God, if he's done anything to my brother, I'll kill him. Let him know that the next time you don't talk to him."

Mac watches him go, then looks at me. "He's freaked out that his brother is missing," he says.

People are staring at us, but I don't care. "I don't know anything," I say to Mac, as if it will make any difference.

He shrugs. "If I were you, I'd keep my head down for a while."

And then he's gone, sucked into the river of kids moving through the hall. And I'm left standing here alone.

I spend the rest of the day wishing I were anywhere else.

As I near my house after school, I notice a circle of journalists outside. I turn quickly down the side street that runs behind my house, pulling my sweatshirt's hood up as I go. I feel like some kind of criminal. There's a car idling at the back of my property. Unfortunately, thanks to the neighbors' fences, there's no other way into my yard.

Keeping my head down, I walk straight at the car. As I'm about to cut into the hole in the hedge, the door opens.

"Lauren." Detective Evans swings out of the car, pulling her sunglasses on as she comes toward me.

"I don't want to talk to you."

"I was hoping that maybe you've heard from your brother."

"I haven't."

"Suspicious, isn't it?"

I stop and look at myself in her glasses. "No, it isn't."

"Does he often stay away from home for days on end?" she asks.

"Maybe he does," I say. "But why would he show up here right now when it seems as though everyone thinks he's abducted Benny?"

"Possibly to let us know he had nothing to do with Benjamin's disappearance."

"And you'd just believe him?"

"We'd simply like to ask him some questions," she says.

I swing my backpack off and set it on the ground. "He's not here. I don't know where he is. He hasn't contacted me.

Now, can you leave us alone?" She doesn't respond, so I go on. "And could you get those reporters away from the front of our house?"

"The journalists are on public property. Nothing I can do about them," she says as she gets back in the cruiser. "This would all be easier if Tom contacted us."

I pick my pack up and cut through the hole in the hedge. When I look back, Detective Evans is still sitting there.

My mother is in front of the television.

"Did they bother you?" she asks.

"The journalists?"

"Yes."

"I came in the back." I decide not to tell her about Detective Evans. "What about you?"

"I came home from work early, just in case."

"Just in case Tom was here?"

"Yes, but of course he isn't. I think they've been out there all day. They've even bothered Joanne."

Joanne is our elderly widowed neighbor. "What did they do?"

"Asked questions about us. About Tom." My mother shakes her head and holds her temples. "This is all so awful."

"I know, Mom," I say, sitting down beside her. We're not a really huggy family, so this is about as consoling as it's going to get.

I lean against her.

"When is it going to end?" she says.

"When Benny comes home," I say.

"Or Tom comes back," she says. "Where is he, Lauren? Where could he have gone?"

I put an arm over her shoulder and pull her to me. "It'll be okay," I promise. As if I can see into the future. As if I know anything at all.

ELEVEN

The screen bangs against the wall as I drop it to the ground. A breeze pushes through the empty space. I climb out the window and onto the lawn. This time I slide the window closed behind me, checking to make certain it didn't somehow lock. I pass beneath the tree house and go directly to the hedge. I've decided on a black hoodie, jeans and thin sandals. I try not to think of anything as I walk. The chilly night air washes over me. Whenever a thought rushes to the front of my mind, I visualize exhaling it in a long single breath. It works for a time, but soon enough there are too many thoughts elbowing one another for space, and the minute I expel them they rush back into the lineup.

About Ben and my brother.

About Erin and how she must be feeling.

I'm five blocks from home when I sense a car behind me. It could have been there for a while—I've been so deep in thought, I might not have noticed. It's a block away, moving slowly.

It has to be Detective Evans again. Following me, hoping I'll lead her to Tom. It bothers me how crafty she thinks she is. Also, how single-minded she is about Tom's guilt. I get angry as I think of all the other things she could be doing with her time. But I guess she's already made up her mind. Tom is guilty.

Period.

I stop at the edge of the park on Helpern. I wait a second, gauging whether the car's driver is watching me. I quickly dart into the park, dashing across the grass and sand toward the woods and down to the ravine.

The little forts have been torn down, leaving nothing but clumps of sticks and dirty blankets that have been tossed in the creek. I find myself beside the massive oak with the climbing boards leading to the lowest branches. I grab a board and pull myself up. It only takes a few seconds to get to the first crotch of the tree. I hold on tightly and wait.

My breathing slows, and I can feel the shot of adrenaline seeping through my neck and shoulders.

A minute later, a figure appears on the cusp of the rise. From the distance, I can't tell who it is. I am trying my best not to move, but the way I am crouching is uncomfortable, and I can feel my thighs cramping.

The figure moves toward me, then stops, and suddenly there are voices.

"Yes, Detective Evans here. Go ahead." Her voice crosses the distance with ease. A cloud shifts, and in the bright moonlight I can see Detective Evans holding a walkie-talkie near her ear. "Affirmative," she says. She turns and starts back up the rise. "Yes, send an officer to my location." She stops, looks back, then goes on.

When I figure she's gone, I climb down. The ground is uneven beneath my sandals. I look up the hill to find a pair of flashlight beams illuminating the trees on the edge of the ravine.

You could have stayed at home, I tell myself as I run across a plank that straddles the creek. I scramble up the bank as the flashlights light up the creek. I slide in behind a tree and then, for some reason, take off running on the other side of the ravine.

My sandals slip from my feet, and I'm about to stop to retrieve them when someone calls out, "Lauren Saunders, is that you? Can you come here for a moment, please?" and I decide to leave my sandals and keep running.

It's stupid. I feel like an idiot, clambering in the dark for no reason. There would be too much explaining to do. Honestly, I'm tired of saying the same thing over and over again.

I don't realize where I am for a moment. A car drives past with a deep, thudding bass rattling its windows.

The clouds part again, and I see the West Tower to my right, know the East is just in the distance over my shoulder, and figure out exactly where I am.

I never come here. Anyone who doesn't live here avoids this area. It's called Maple Grove and was supposed to be an "ideal community." Somewhere in the process the builders changed their minds and threw up a bunch of two- and three-story co-op places with a scattering of row houses, then disappeared. A few years later someone else came along and erected the two largest towers in the city on either side of the community, making it feel like something dark and evil from Middle Earth.

The whole area is rental units. There were supposed to be gardens in the center of each block, but all that grows in this area is weeds.

Speaking of which, weed is also the number-one export from Maple Grove. One industrious seller packaged his baggies with a Maple Grove sticker left over from when the towers were first built. They say, *Maple Grove, high above the ordinary.*

I cross my arms over my chest, tuck my head into the collar of my hoodie and start walking.

I've made it two blocks when a police car crosses the street ahead of me and slows. Without thinking, I turn onto a walkway that runs between two of the housing units and take off down the path, dodging garbage cans and abandoned tricycles.

"What were you doing?" I say out loud. My thigh muscles are twitching from the run. At any moment I could step on something sharp and slice a foot open, but I'm too scared to care. I turn in the direction I think will get me back out toward a main road and then slow to a walk.

As I'm passing a doorway, a group of guys comes barreling out, laughing and punching one another. I walk faster but not so fast as to seem intimidated.

"Hey, who that?" one of them says.

I keep walking, my breath coming in little gulps.

"Yo, that a girl or a dude? Hey, you a girl or a dude?"

I don't look back.

"Ain't answering," someone else says in a high, nasal voice.

"You know who that is?"

"No, man. Let's find out."

I'm almost to the street when they catch me.

One of the guys gets an arm around me just as I'm gaining some speed.

"It's a girl. What you doin' here, girl?" He's older than I am, mid-twenties maybe. He has a wispy mustache and crooked teeth. He turns me around so I'm facing the other two guys. One of them is tall and, I'd say were the situation different, handsome. The other guy is large in that way people are once they've given up on all physical fitness.

"You like her?" the guy holding me says. He's swaying and shifting but still holding me tightly. The stink of alcohol and pot wafts off them.

"Who, me?" the fat guy says.

The guy holding me laughs, and something wet hits my neck. "Yeah, whatcha think?"

I finally gather up enough courage to struggle, twisting in his grip. "Let go of me."

I'm about to scream when the guy holding me throws a hand over my mouth and drags me back against the side of the building. I try to bite his hand, but he shifts and I get nothing but air. He's holding my chin so I can't move my jaw at all. "We were about to go out and get you laid," he says to the fat guy. "This is like a gift from the gods or something. What do you think?"

"She don't wanna be with me," the fat guy says. He's got a tall can of beer in his hand. He takes a long drink before wiping his mouth on his sleeve. "Does she?"

"I don't think we're askin'." The guy laughs again.

The fat guy screws his face up. "I ain't so sure about that. Weren't we just gonna go find Connie? Your old man says—"

"Sure, sure, but you want to go where my old man's already been?"

"No, it's..." the fat guy says. "This ain't right."

"It'd be free." The guy laughs again, then belches into my ear.

I try to get my leg up behind me to kick him in the groin, but he shifts to the side, still laughing like it's all some awesome game. Without even looking at him, I can tell he's glassy-eyed drunk. The kind of intoxicated people get where a strange belief takes over them that nothing they do will ever have any consequences. I've been there; I understand the feeling.

Which scares me all the more.

The handsome guy hasn't said a word. He's taken a cigarette out and is looking at the street. I try to kick again, and the guy holding me wraps a leg around mine and holds me tightly with his free hand.

"Man, I don't think so," the fat guy says.

The handsome guy suddenly walks away.

"Where you goin', Jones?"

"I don't want anything to do with this. Pretend it never happened."

"Whatever, man. I'm only fooling around." He moves his face so I can see him. "What do you think of my friend Artie here? You think he's hot?" The guy forces my head up and down. "See, Artie, she thinks you're hot. Like Leonardo DiCaprio, right?" My head is forced up and down again. The fat guy smiles as if he's buying into this, and I can picture him on top of me. Can see it all from beginning to end. And while I'm picturing this, while I'm waiting for this nightmare to kick into high gear, the guy holding me lets go, and a moment later he's spun around, holding his hand.

"What the hell?" he says. There's blood gushing from a cut on his palm and wrist.

"Start walking," a new voice says from behind me.

"Whoa, buddy, what the hell?" the fat guy says. He takes a step forward, and I feel the guy behind me dart out. A moment later the fat guy is cradling his hand. Drips of blood stain the concrete beneath us.

"You gotta move, Lauren." I look up, half expecting it to be Tom, even though the voice is much deeper than my brother's.

"Who are you?" I say.

"Grady," he says. He turns around and walks backward.

"Dude," the guy who was holding me says, "I am going to kill you."

"I will cut you faster than you can blink!" Grady says. The guy takes a step forward, and Grady flashes the knife at him.

"I'm a friend of Tom's," Grady says. His voice quivers.

"There's two of us, dude," the first guy says.

"I'm really bleeding," the fat one says. He's holding his hand, and there's blood dripping on the ground all around him.

"We're going to run now," Grady says. He gives me a little shove.

"Don, I gotta get someone to look at this," I hear the big guy say, and with that they move from the light and back into the building.

When we get to the sidewalk, where the streetlights shine more brightly, I take a closer look at Grady. He's tall, around six feet, and thin. He's wearing a tie, a white dress shirt and jeans. His hair is flicked up at the front and trimmed on the sides.

He steps away from me once we're out in the open. "My car is up here." He looks back at the building. "Those guys are pissed. I really don't think we should hang out here for long."

"You're friends with Tom?" I ask.

"Yes."

I'm shaking. "How can I know that?" I ask.

Grady stops beside a dilapidated Honda Civic and opens the front passenger door. "His favorite flavor of ice cream is cookies and cream. He used to play soccer before he put on weight. He still watches every episode of *The Simpsons* no matter how bad it is. And we really, *really* need to not be here right now."

All of this is true. *The Simpsons* was one of the few things we'd talk about every week. If our father didn't drop Tom off, he'd call and we'd go over the episode from beginning to end, charting the characters' lives.

"I mean, even if they aren't coming back, those guys could call the cops. I did assault them."

"You were saving me," I say. "No one would blame you."

"I have the weapon." He looks at the building again. "I don't want to leave you here. Tom would be seriously pissed if I did. But I'm not going to force you to do anything you don't want to. And by that I only mean getting in my car. Like, going with me to try to find your brother."

"You think you know where he is?" I say.

"Not for sure, no. But maybe."

"Where?" I say.

"I'll show you," Grady replies. "If you can trust me."

TWELVE

As we cross the bridge, I press myself to the door and pull my legs up onto the seat.

I don't know this guy. I would say, looking at him, that he's harmless. But he just cut two people with a knife, so maybe *harmless* is the wrong word.

"Are you okay?" he asks. The streetlights are brighter here, set up on giant towers in the median. The inside of the car flares up, then fades to gray every few seconds as we pass from one halo of light to another.

"Sure," I say, though I don't even sound convincing to myself.

"That must have freaked you out a bit."

"Um, yeah. And you too. Are you okay?"

"I'm good. I do that kind of shit every day," Grady says, doing a little head-shiver thing.

"Oh, do you?"

"Fo' sure, girl," he says through his laughter. "Actually, that scared the hell out of me. I didn't mean to cut that guy who was holding you."

"So what happened?"

"I just meant to get the knife out and, I don't know, wave it around. I kept thinking, *Brandish it, Grady. That'll be enough.* But I got too close and accidentally cut him. He also moved in to me, if we're being honest."

"Oh, of course, and if we're being honest, what about the other guy?"

"He was an easy mark. But again, I only meant to get close. I know it might be hard to believe, but I've never done anything like that before."

"That's what they all say."

"Seriously," Grady goes on. He holds his hand out, and it is shaking almost as bad as mine. "See, that totally freaked me out."

I hold my hand up beside his. "We match," I say.

I try to slow my breathing and in doing so detect an inexplicable odor. I look at the floor, then into the backseat. A laptop lies half out of an open backpack, alongside four cell phones in a Tupperware container. I sniff loudly.

"Yeah, about that smell," Grady says. "This isn't my car."

"Oh, whose is it?" I clasp one hand with the other, but the shaking continues. My throat feels as if it has needles in it. Grady seems calm. Which worries me even more.

"My uncle owns an auto-wrecking place." Grady glances at me. "People bring cars in they don't think work but really only need an adjustment or a couple of replacement parts. That happens because, basically, people are lazy. I mean, it's a car, right? Who decides their car is ready for the wrecker without first getting it seriously checked out? Anyway, my uncle keeps some extra license plates around, so if I can fix a car, I can take it out."

"Oh." I sniff again for effect. "Any idea what that is?"

"It's rancid, isn't it? I didn't notice it until I turned the air-conditioning on."

The windows are down, and a hard wind pushes through the car. It's the beginning of June, and the weather has already turned from spring to summer. Resurrection Falls is far enough north, right up near the Canadian border, that we get really distinct seasons.

"Let's leave that off then," I say.

Grady laughs. He's tall enough that his head almost brushes the ceiling.

"Where do you think he is?" I ask, trying to change the topic.

"It's just a guess, but we sometimes jam in this old warehouse by the lake."

"Jam?" I say. "As in play music?"

"Yeah, I have a portable studio. We bring a guitar and a few drums and set up in there. The sound is amazing."

"What does Tom play?" We stop at an intersection. Cars flash past. Music pours from the speakers outside a McDonald's. It's after midnight, and most of the city is asleep.

"You don't know?" Grady says.

"No, I didn't know he could play any instrument."

"He sings."

"Is he good?"

"He's great." The light changes and Grady pulls through the intersection. "He's never told you? Or, like, you've never heard him singing at home? He's crazy talented. It's really annoying."

"We kind of move in our own circles."

Grady says, "He did mention that."

"How do you know him?"

"I used to work at the record shop downtown before it closed. You know that one on Percy Street? Radicals?"

"No," I say. "I didn't know record shops still existed." We are out of the city limits now, heading for the warehouse district.

"That was the last one. Your brother would come in and listen to soul albums."

"Really?" I say, trying not to sound too surprised.

"Yeah, he loves that old soul stuff. Some blues as well." Grady glances at me. "He has that old-school voice. I guess you don't know that."

"I've never heard him hum, never mind sing."

"I found out he could sing by accident. One day I had to run down the street to grab something, and I left him in the store by himself. But I'd forgotten my wallet and had to go right back. When I came in, I thought it was an old Smokey Robinson or Sam Cooke a capella thing playing. But it was your brother, wearing headphones and singing along. After that I became the most aggravating person alive, trying to get him to jam with me. He finally caved, but only if we were somewhere no one could hear him. Which is why we started coming out here."

"What do you play?" I ask.

"A bit of everything. Drums, keyboards, guitar. Absolutely no singing."

"Do you go to Mitchell Mayer?"

"My mom pulled me out of regular school in the eighth grade. Since then I've been homeschooled. But not really. My mom started doing a few things with me, and eventually, I guess, she figured I would learn everything I could about anything I am interested in and left me to it. I passed my GED last year."

Outside, the old, abandoned manufacturing plants and warehouses rise up in the darkness.

"Listen, if you're nervous coming in here with me, that's okay. You don't have to. You can wait in the car, or I can take you home now. You don't really know me or anything. I can tell you I'm not a creepy guy, but how would you know for sure?"

"What's with the tie?" I ask.

Grady flips his tie. "That's complicated," he says. "Basically, I've discovered that if you look like a criminal, people think you're a criminal. Whereas a guy wearing a tie is on his way somewhere important." He smiles at me, then pulls off the highway onto a secondary road.

There's a drop of blood on his white shirt, which instantly gives me the shivers again. I hate blood.

"Where are your shoes?" he asks.

"That's kind of a personal question," I say.

"Is it?"

"No, I'm joking. They fell off when I was scrambling around in that stupid ravine."

"Oh." He palms the steering wheel. "What were you doing in the ravine?"

"I was climbing trees," I say.

"Nice," he says. "Do you have a cell phone?"

I hold my phone up for him to see.

"Yeah, of course you do. Dumb question." He pulls in between a set of Dumpsters and a very tall fence around the back of the warehouse.

"Okay. So. How about you keep your phone in your hand and, I don't know, stay a bit away from me when we walk in? Whatever makes you comfortable." He shuts the car off, and a silence envelops us.

"Comfortable," I say. I look at all the dark corners and imagine sitting in the car with my mind going crazy.

Grady nods and gives me a really forced smile.

"That's creepy."

"What?"

"Your smile. Why does your face do that?" Which is totally rude. I sometimes get like this. Saying whatever comes into my head. Usually when I'm nervous.

"I don't know how to smile. Class photos are probably the main reason I left institutionalized public education. I mean..." He smiles again. "Seriously? Who can't smile?"

"Maybe say something when you smile. I hear that helps."

"What do you mean?"

"Like cheese, but not cheese. Something that makes you laugh. Then your smile will be genuine."

"Gastromancy!" Grady says, laughing.

"What does that mean?"

"It's the telling of fortunes by listening to someone's stomach grumblings."

"That's ridiculous."

He laughs, and his smile is nice.

"But it works," I tell him. I figure a guy who knows what gastromancy is can't be that evil.

"So, are you coming?"

I rub the side of my cell phone. I light up the screen and notice that my battery is half dead, which makes no sense. My phone normally lasts all day, and I could swear I had it plugged in for a while at home as well.

"Into this dark, abandoned building with you?" I say.

Grady looks at the building. "Yeah. Seriously, though, no pressure. You can stay here. Even keep the keys. Whatever."

For some reason, an idea I should have had when this whole thing began strikes me for the first time. "Why were you there?" I ask.

"Why was I where?"

"Maple Grove. What were you doing there?"

Grady looks out the window. "I was following you," he says. He puts his hand on the key again. "Listen, I'm going to take you home right now. I can come back and—"

"Why were you following me?" I say.

He sighs as though about to tell me some deep secret.

"I've been trying to figure out where Tom is. Then that whole thing happened with the kid. Of course, I was certain there was no way Tom had anything to do with it. But I didn't know anyone else he might have talked to other than you. So I was hanging around your area trying to build up the nerve to knock or, I guess, hoping Tom might just show up."

"And when Tom didn't show up, you decided to just follow me?"

"I wasn't going to let you know I was following you," Grady says, then shakes his head again. "That sounds even more creepy."

"Um, yeah," I say.

"I'm worried about your brother, and I want to know if he's all right. I probably didn't go about this the right way, but I'm still figuring it all out as well. So if you want me to take you home, cool, I'll do that. If not, let's go see if he's inside." He reaches into the backseat, pulls a flashlight out of the backpack, then opens his door and gets out.

I sit there for a moment. I hold my hand out before me and find it's no longer shaking. Grady is fiddling with the flashlight. He gives it a quick tap, and it comes to life.

I leave my hand on the door handle for a moment before opening the door, getting out and walking toward him.

"Do you want a pair of shoes or something?" he asks.

"You have extra girls' shoes in your car?" I say.

"That would be creepy. I have a pair of running shoes in the backseat. They'll be really big on you, but at least you won't step on a piece of rusted metal in your bare feet."

I open up the back door and dig around beneath the seat. My hand finds the shoes, and I bring them out. They're at least two sizes too big.

Grady says, "Try leaning forward when you walk."

I take a couple of steps, and the backs flap against the ground.

"You could be starting a new style here," Grady says. "Who knows."

THIRTEEN

Grady's flashlight is insufficient in the wide open space of the warehouse. We can only see a few feet in front of us at any time, leaving the rest of the area a complete mystery. There'd been a piece of duct tape over the lock on one door. Grady had been careful to make certain the tape stayed in place once we were inside.

"Stay close to the walls," Grady says. The giant shoes bang with each step. I try shuffling for a moment, but this seems to make more noise.

"Where do you and Tom jam?" I whisper.

"In the next room." He flicks the flashlight beam toward a door at the end of the space. Our footsteps cause riots of noise. There are so many dark spots. I wish Grady would move the flashlight around more, just in case someone is in the room. It feels like the perfect place for a homeless guy to live. I've had enough of those kinds of surprises for a while.

"Is it weird in there?" I ask.

"What do you mean by weird? It's a room like this one. Pretty big and open." Even though we are both whispering, it seems like our voices are bouncing off the walls and ceiling, amplifying as they come back at us.

"When were you here last?"

"One week and three days ago," Grady says with authority. "We worked on 'A Change Is Gonna Come.'"

"What's that?"

"A Sam Cooke song. One of his best."

"Okay, I'll trust you on that." Grady opens a door and we enter a new part of the warehouse. The space is strangely arranged. There isn't any consistency to the size of the rooms.

"I wish he had a cell we could call," Grady says.

"Do you find that weird?" I ask. Talking is making me feel more comfortable.

"The cell thing? Not really. It doesn't feel as if Tom is really a part of this era. He's like a time traveler from the fifties. He seems to operate outside of the modern world."

"He doesn't use computers either."

"Sure he does," Grady says. "I loaned him a laptop. He does most of the setup and stuff for recording as well."

"He has a laptop?" I try to picture Tom tapping away at a keyboard and can't.

"My uncle collects old computers, and we get them working again. I offered one to Tom, but he said he didn't have a use for it outside of recording." Grady reaches out and opens the door to the next room. Something scurries away in the darkness, and I grab his arm. "It's cool," he says. "There are some mice in here. But they disappear as soon as we show."

"That's not cool," I say. I look behind me. I thought I heard something there, coming in the door. Or moving, slithering across the floor.

"Mice don't hurt people."

"They're gross," I say.

"That's one opinion," he says.

"Don't tell me you have mice as pets or something weird like that."

"I do not have mice as pets. But I assume they should be granted the ability to thrive in places humans have deserted. It's only natural."

"Natural," I say.

We step in. Moonlight softens the floorboards in great circles. The ceiling seems miles above us. The wind has picked up outside, creating a low moaning. "Right over here," Grady says, directing the flashlight beam to a corner of the room where a lone water bottle sits on a table between two chairs.

"I don't remember leaving this," Grady says, picking it up. Though the room is large, this little area with the chairs and table seems close and intimate. I can almost imagine

Tom being here, inhabiting this space. Though I still can't imagine him singing.

"What were you expecting to find?" I ask. The room feels really close, even though it's huge. The air is dense and flat, still holding a bit of the day's heat.

"Tom," he says.

"Like, living here?" I'm about to sit down on one of the chairs when there's a banging in the other room. Grady puts a finger to his lips and switches off his flashlight.

At first we hear nothing more, but then there's the unmistakable sound of footsteps. The door between the rooms is open, and a moment later a bright flashlight beam cracks the darkness.

"Do you think it's him?" I whisper.

Grady grabs my hand, pulling me with him toward the far wall. As he's passing the second chair, he stops, leans down and picks something up from the floor. Suddenly, his lips brush my ear as he whispers, "If it's not him, we're right beside a door."

"How will we know?" I whisper back. The flashlight beam grows in both size and strength.

"Wait," Grady says. The beam shifts, and we hear an endless stream of numbers and letters pouring from what sounds like a police radio. It grows louder before falling silent.

"Cops," I say. Grady opens the door, pulls me through and silently shuts it.

We're on the other side of the warehouse and have to double back around. As we turn the corner, I spot a police car parked beside the neighboring building.

"There's a cruiser," I say, grabbing Grady's arm. We hug the wall of the warehouse until we can be certain no one is inside the cruiser. I slide back into the shadows, bringing Grady with me. "Don't they usually work in pairs?" I say.

"There's likely another one around here somewhere."

We move around Dumpsters and garbage bags, staying away from the few remaining lights as much as possible. I begin to run toward the car, and one of Grady's too-big shoes slips off my foot. I trip and go down. It seems as if I've barely hit the ground before I feel Grady's hands beneath my arms, lifting me back up.

"You okay?" he says.

I glance down at my knees, which seem fine. "I'm okay."

He lets me go, and we cover the rest of the distance to the car. Grady stops on the passenger side and opens the door for me.

"How did anyone know we were there?" I say.

Grady gets in the car, starts the engine and backs out into the lot.

"That couldn't have been random," I say. "Why would the police patrol this area?"

"I doubt they would," Grady says. "This would be rent-a-cop territory, if anything."

Rocks ping off the tires, and to my ears it sounds like a fireworks display. Instead of retracing our route past the warehouse, he drives around the back to a service entrance that connects to the next set of buildings.

"Have the police questioned you?" Grady asks.

"I spent all of yesterday with a detective. Why?"

He glances down at my hands; I'm rubbing the sides of my cell phone again. "Have you had your phone with you all the time?"

I think back through everything that's happened. "Every second."

"Did you ever leave it anywhere?"

I think again and remember leaving the phone in Detective Evans's car when the two of us walked to the school, looking for Ben. I'd set it on the seat while I juggled the food and coffee, and in my hungover haze had forgotten to retrieve it. "I left it in this detective's car," I say. "Detective Evans."

"Let me see it," Grady says. I hand my phone over to him, and he flicks through it, keeping one eye on the road.

"Maybe you should pull over while you do that," I say.

He slows almost to a stop and hands the phone back to me.

"Right here," he says.

On the screen is an app called *trackme*.

"It can be hidden," he explains as we pull back out onto the street connecting the warehouses with the highway.

"It's mostly for people who are paranoid about losing their phones and parents wanting to virtually creep their kids."

"She had this installed on my phone?" I say in disbelief. "Why would she do that?"

"She must believe you know where Tom is and aren't telling."

"But that's illegal, right? The police can't track anyone they like."

"Very illegal. But unless you saw her put it on, you can't prove that she did," Grady says. "On the other hand, they can't ever admit to having put it on either."

There is a gas-station complex just before the highway ramp. Grady pulls in beside the little store, parks beyond the reach of the neon lights and brings the laptop out from the backseat. "Let me see that again," he says.

I hand him my phone. He looks back and forth between the two screens, typing madly on the laptop while flicking through screens on my phone.

"She didn't know about the Tom connection until..." I begin, and then I remember how Detective Evans had been texting someone as we walked back to the cruiser. And how she'd been asking me questions about Tom at the same time. There's every chance that she had the other officer go into her cruiser and install the app on my phone. I never password-protect my phone because I hate having to type something in every time I use it. Of course, with her penetrating stare, she would have noticed me forgetting it in her car.

"There, that's better," Grady says, turning the laptop toward me. "You're now hurtling down the highway away from town. If they are tracking you in real time, we should see the cruiser go past any minute."

"How'd you do that?"

"These programs are easy. Whoever installed it used a password, so it might take a few minutes to crack that when we want to remove the program."

"I didn't see it at first," I say, staring at him.

"See what?" He looks all innocent and timid.

"That you're a giant nerd," I say, laughing.

"I told you, when I get interested in something, I learn all I can about it."

"And you're interested in hacking?"

"I'm interested in computers. Hacking is the devil on your shoulder. The apple of knowledge. The—"

"Okay, okay, I get it. With knowledge comes power, and you have to decide how to use that power."

"There's the cruiser," Grady says, pointing at a set of headlights. "See if you recognize the driver."

I squint at the cruiser as it passes but can't make out the driver through the tinted windows. "It's a regular cop car," I say. "Detective Evans was in an unmarked one."

"She sent her lackey," Grady says. He's typing on the keyboard again. "You want me to remove that app now?"

I think about this for a second, then say, "You can do that whenever, right?"

"Sure."

"And with the laptop, you can make them think I'm somewhere else?"

"Wherever you want to be."

"So let's leave it. This could be fun."

Grady laughs. "Now who's the degenerate?" He tosses the laptop into the backseat and pulls a book out of his pocket.

"What's that?"

"It's the book your brother was reading last time we were at the warehouse." He holds it up. It's called A Confederacy of Dunces. "I found it on the floor near the door."

"That means he was there recently, right?"

"Not necessarily. He might have forgotten it at our last jam session."

We both look at the book.

"Where the hell are you, Tom?" Grady says under his breath.

FOURTEEN

There's something strange about the front of my house.

At first I can't tell what it is, but then a bit of motion catches my eye. The curtain is blowing in the breeze. The problem is that it's blowing outside, because most of the window is no longer there.

"What's going on with your window?" Grady says, shutting off the engine.

"I don't know."

"It wasn't like that before?"

I stare at him. "Yeah, this is how we leave our place all the time."

"Want me to come in with you?"

I consider saying no.

"Yes," I say. "Yeah, that'd be good." I open the door and say, "Mom?"

"I flick the living room light on and stand in the hallway, listening. Grady is right behind me.

"Should she be here?" he asks.

"She is. But she takes these pills for her migraines that totally knock her out."

I step into the living room and find a brick on the floor, lying amid the broken glass. I bend over to pick it up, and Grady stops me.

"Leave it. In case there are fingerprints. Look, there's a note." He bends down, pulls a pen out of his pocket and flicks a piece of paper that is tied to the brick.

Tell us where he is, it reads.

"Any idea who would have done this?" Grady asks.

I say, "Ben's stepbrother JJ is convinced Tom took Ben."

"If that app on your phone means anything, that's what the police believe as well."

"As well as the news reports, which mention Tom by name."

"Yeah, those don't help."

"Did you turn off the misdirection for that app?"

"It reverts back to the phone's true location eventually."

"Let me check on my mom, and then I'll call the police."

Grady rubs at the back of his head and inhales deeply.

"Don't worry," I tell him. "You can leave before they get here."

"It's not like I'm a criminal or anything. But with the car and the plates and..."

"Don't worry, I understand." I walk down the hall to my mom's room and open the door. She's fallen asleep with her light on. I get close enough to listen to her slow, shallow breathing.

"Okay," I say to Grady when I return to the living room. "You're free." I pull out my cell. "But you'd better get going. I have a feeling it won't be long before the good detective arrives."

"Yeah, for sure," Grady says. He gives me another genuine smile. It's adorable.

"Well done," I say.

"What?"

"That was an awesome smile. It felt real."

"Oh, thanks." He steps out the door. "I'll text you if I can think of anywhere else your brother might be."

"Won't you need my number for that?"

"I already have it," he says. "Be careful where you go with that app on."

"What if I need to get a hold of you?" Suddenly, I don't want him to leave. I've only just met him, but I feel somehow safer with him in my life.

Grady reaches into his pocket, pulls his phone out and hits a few numbers. A moment later my cell buzzes.

The text reads **Grade-D**.

"Nerd," I say.

"For life," he replies, making some kind of hand gesture I don't understand.

I call 9-1-1 as I watch him drive away.

— — — —

Detective Evans arrives within ten minutes, with a uniformed officer in tow.

"Do you have any idea who would do this?" she asks, kneeling beside the brick. The army of crickets camped in our front garden is chirping. The noise is eerie as it floats in the broken window. The officer looks around the room like he's come to an open-house showing.

"By the note, I guess it would be someone who believes Tom has something to do with Benny's disappearance." I sit on the couch and cross my arms. Detective Evans removes an evidence bag from her pocket and hands it to the officer.

"Get the lab to check for fingerprints." The officer bags the brick, then stands there as if more evidence is suddenly going to jump out at him.

"I'll go take a look outside," he eventually says, leaving Detective Evans and me alone.

"Was there anyone home when this occurred?"

"My mother."

"Where is she now?"

"Sleeping," I say.

Detective Evans raises an eyebrow and leans to look down the hall. "Through all of this?"

"She takes medication for severe migraines, and it totally knocks her out."

She opens her notepad. "And where were you?"

"Out," I say. "Are there any leads on Benny?"

"Not at the moment, no. Where did you say you were tonight?"

"I didn't." I can tell she's waiting for me to lie to her. "Have you considered letting the public know that Tom had nothing to do with Ben's disappearance? Maybe he's just scared because he figures the police are out to get him."

"We need to talk to him, Lauren."

"Then stop putting his picture on TV next to Ben's. You know how it looks. And other people have obviously gotten the wrong idea as well."

"That decision is out of my hands."

The door opens and the officer steps back in. "Detective, I have some footprints out here. Should I get CSI to come and take some molds?"

Detective Evans stares at me. "You have no idea who could have thrown that brick through your window?"

"No," I lie.

Detective Evans inhales slowly. "No one has spoken to you about this situation?"

I could tell her I think it's JJ. But I know it won't do any good. She already showed her allegiance to the Carters when she didn't step in between JJ and me earlier. I would look petty, I'm certain, and if she ever approached JJ with this accusation, he would make up some lie about me. Something I'd said or done that proves I'm not to be trusted. So I just shake my head.

"Okay," she says to the officer. "Let's get a mold." The officer tips his hat and closes the door. "Maybe we should go over this again, Lauren. When did you last see your brother?"

"Saturday."

"And where was that?"

"He stopped by the park where Ben and I were playing."

"Did he say anything to Benjamin Carter?"

"He would have said hello. I don't remember anything else."

"Think, Lauren. Think about where you were standing when your brother approached. Where Benjamin was."

No one calls him Benjamin. I want to scream at Detective Evans every time she does. "Benny was on the platform of the play structure," I say. "I was at the bottom of the slide. Tom came from the road and walked across the sand."

"Okay. And what did he say?"

I close my eyes. "*Hi.*"

"And then?"

"We talked about—"

"No, tell me what he said. Exactly," she says sharply.

"How am I supposed to remember that? It was days ago. It was just a conversation."

"Try for me, Lauren. It could be very important. If you have to, put yourself above the scene. Try and see it like it's a movie playing. Or you're a bird looking down on it."

I give that a shot. It feels ridiculous.

"He said, *How long have you guys been here?* and I said, *Half an hour.* Then Ben came down the slide and Tom said, *Hi, Benny, how are you doing today?* And Ben said, *I'm well. Thank you for asking.*"

"That's exactly what he said?"

"Yes."

"Does Benjamin always talk like that?"

"Yes. His mother is crazy about his manners. In a good way."

"And your brother calls him Benny?"

"Anyone who really knows him does," I say, feeling a sense of familiarity with Ben that Detective Evans will never have. "His friends."

"Okay. Go on. What happened next?"

"Benny went back to the structure."

"And what did your brother do?"

"He asked me—"

"What were his words, Lauren? Exactly what he asked," she says, way too sharply.

"I don't know!" I yell. "I can't remember everything *exactly*. This is like a nothing moment in my life. Tom was walking by, he saw us, he came to say hi. He asked what I was doing that night, and then he left. He kept walking."

"Why did he ask what you were doing that night?"

"Because he's my brother? Because that's what people do?"

"You told me before that you two were not close. That you didn't have much to do with one another. That you ran in different circles. You said all these things."

"Oh my god, that doesn't mean he wouldn't stop and talk to me."

"Where was he coming from?" Detective Evans asks.

"I don't know. I didn't ask."

"Where was he going?"

"I don't know. I don't know any of this. That was the entire encounter!"

"Okay, Lauren. Okay. I'm sorry you are so upset."

"Sorry? Really? You think my brother has, like, abducted a kid. That he's some sick pervert who—"

"We don't necessarily…"

"—is going to do weird things to him. You think he's this giant freak. Why? Because he was in the neighborhood that night? Because he once asked some kid about a sand castle? Because he doesn't have a cell phone? You think you have him all figured out, but you don't know him at all. You have no idea."

"You're right, Lauren, I don't know your brother. I've never met him. I'm going on what I have. There's some kind of a connection here between Tom and Benjamin Carter. The closed-circuit videos from the grocery store have us asking a lot of questions. What was Tom doing there? Why was he connecting with Benjamin? Why not talk to Erin? But the biggest question remains, what was Tom doing outside the mayor's house the night Benjamin disappeared, and where did he go? We need to talk to your brother about all of this. Just talk, Lauren. Nothing more."

"You don't know Tom," I say. "He wouldn't ever do anything. You don't know him at all."

Detective Evans stands. "I think you need to ask yourself, Lauren, how well do *you* know your brother?"

"Better than…"

Detective Evans holds her hand up, and for some reason I stop speaking. Like it's not my house. Like I'm not in the right. Like I'm nothing but a stupid kid who has no idea what is going on in the big bad world.

"*Really* know him, Lauren. Stand outside of everything you think you know about your brother. All the memories and time spent together. Stand outside all of that and look at him as we are. And then tell me, how well do you know him right now?"

"I know him," I say. "I can't step outside all of that because he's my brother and I know him."

"So where is he?" Detective Evans opens the door. "Please call us if you think of anything about Benjamin, or if Tom contacts you."

As she's closing the door, I yell, "No one calls him Benjamin!"

FIFTEEN

TUESDAY

I'm halfway to school on Tuesday morning when I notice what looks like an unmarked police car following me. There's every chance I'm being paranoid. With reason, of course. But I turn down an alley anyway and pop out on the street behind the school rather than in front of it. I sit down on a bench and pretend to be looking at my phone. Sure enough, half a minute later the same car rolls past, sporting tinted windows and those little police-issued hubcaps.

I stand as it passes, my head still down. I text Grady: **Need to meet with you.**

I begin walking back around to the front of the school. I'm almost at the side door when my phone buzzes. There's a text from a number I don't recognize.

Starbucks, 5th and Main, twenty min? G.

K, L., I text back, then slip my phone into a pocket and enter the school.

— — — —

"I thought I could do it," I tell the school office administrator, Mrs. Rankin. "But after all that's happened..."

"Oh, I know, dear," Mrs. Rankin replies. Of course she knows. Everyone knows everything. My family is an open book as far as people are concerned. The freak son. The daughter who used to be so good, but now...

"And last night someone threw a brick through my window. I think I should be home with my mom."

"Of course you should," Mrs. Rankin says. "I'll inform your teachers. You go home. Be with your family."

"Thank you."

As I'm leaving, I spot JJ Carter. Luckily, he doesn't see me. He has his hand on a locker, blocking in Katie White. Katie is smiling, but I've heard her talk about how JJ scares her. How he's too aggressive sometimes, and even though she *likes him and everything*, she can't see herself ever dating him.

I keep my head down, clutching my backpack to my chest, hoping I don't see anyone who feels the need for a conversation. The bell rings, and the halls are a cacophony of motion. By the time I push through the front doors, the school sounds as though it might explode behind me.

Outside, I feel an unbelievable sense of freedom. I inhale deeply. It's warm and sunny, and the very thought of being inside a classroom is torture.

The Starbucks is a fifteen-minute walk away. I look behind me now and then, expecting to see the unmarked car. When I don't, I wonder if whoever is tracking me went off to do some actual work after I entered the school.

Starbucks is filled with a midmorning mom-and-kid crowd. There are strollers everywhere and tired-looking women exchanging longer-than-necessary hugs.

"A large coffee, please," I say, defying the Starbucks ridiculous size designation.

The girl behind the counter examines me, then says, "Lauren?"

I don't know who she is. "Um, yeah."

"Grady asked me to take your phone. And for you to meet him around back."

"Oh," I say, looking down at my phone. "Really?"

"I promise I won't do anything with it."

The girl has thick round earrings, and colorful tattoos creeping around the edge of her blouse. Her hair is streaked with purple.

"Okay."

She hands me a coffee, and I slip my phone across the counter to her.

"This place will be packed for the next couple of hours," the girl whispers.

"Okay," I say, though I'm not certain why this matters.

I thank her and back away from the counter. I squeeze past a couple of mothers jiggling their babies and step out into the back alley.

An old Ford Fiesta pulls up, and the front passenger door opens. I lean down to look inside.

"Come on," Grady says.

"What's with all the spy stuff?"

"Hurry," he says.

I get into the car and Grady pulls away as I'm closing the door. "This one smells okay," I say. Grady signals left, away from the Starbucks. As we pull into the intersection, I spot the unmarked cruiser idling across the street.

Grady sniffs. "Just a hint of wet dog."

"So, seriously, what's with all the cloak-and-dagger stuff?"

"You're being followed, right?"

"Sure, but why couldn't you meet me inside? And handing my phone over to that girl...who is she?"

Grady shifts in his seat, sighing heavily. "Look, here's the thing. I'm, um, known to the police."

"Oh," I say. My hand goes to the door handle.

"Not because I'm a degenerate, but because my dad's in jail."

I say, "Okay."

"You're not going to ask what for?" He glances at me.

"You're not your dad. So...whatever."

"I'll tell you anyway. Drunk driving. Hit a pedestrian. Pedestrian died. Dad drives away."

"Hmmm," I say.

"He claims he didn't hit anyone. I believe him. I mean, he shouldn't have been driving drunk. Obviously."

"Obviously."

"But if he'd known he'd hit someone, he would have stopped. He's not some asshole who doesn't take responsibility for his actions. There's a real chance it wasn't him. Like, there was a dent on the car, but they couldn't really prove that it was made by the guy he allegedly hit."

"So why is he in jail?" I ask.

"Someone claimed to have seen the whole thing happen. But my dad was driving a Civic. Everyone drives Civics. It was a Friday night, so there were tons of cars out."

"Oh."

"Yeah. So that's awesome." We drive in silence for a minute. "And also I might have been busted for hacking once."

I don't respond. Grady glances at me, then does that shoulder-shrug thing again.

"It was stupid. I was trying to reset the heat and lights at my middle school. Just to see if I could do it. I didn't want to go to school that day, so I tried to jack the heat to sauna levels."

"You were hacking into a school's computers when you were in the eighth grade?"

"Seventh. Luckily, the police figured I was smart, but not that smart, and they let it go. After that I learned how to not get caught."

"Okay," I say. "Do you have any pets?"

"Pets?"

"Cat or dog or ferret or whatever?"

"Two cats," Grady says.

"Are they okay?"

"What?"

"Like, no one has ever put them in a microwave or bent a little paw too far?"

"What? No."

"Okay, good."

Grady shakes his head. "Why are you asking about my cats?"

"Because I've heard psychopaths usually start out messing around with Fluffy or Patches before moving on to humans. If your cats are all right, then things should be okay for me."

"You're really out there," Grady says after a pause.

"I've heard that before," I say. The sun is warming the car in a nice way. Even the slight hint of wet dog is all right.

"So what did you want to talk about?" Grady stops the car in front of a park. The few mothers who aren't packed into a Starbucks are here, watching their kids eat sand.

I take a long drink of coffee and remember what the homeless guy said about the sweetness of the heat hitting your tongue and the top of your mouth. "Detective Evans totally believes Tom had something to do with Ben's disappearance."

"That seems to be the assumption," Grady says.

"Have you thought of anywhere else Tom might be?"

"We mostly hung out at the warehouse and the record store."

"How did you arrange that?" I say, hand-cranking my window down. "Tom doesn't have a cell or anything. Did you call my house?"

"No, I don't even know the number. Tom would stop by the wrecker's and we'd set up a time, or, if I wasn't busy, we'd just go over."

"He never called you?"

"No," Grady says. "When I didn't see him for a while, I would worry. I'd start to think something had happened. Then he'd show up and we'd play music."

A kid falls off a play structure, and five mothers run to the scene. "He could be anywhere now," I say.

We sit in silence, me looking out the window at the kids on the play structure, Grady gazing at a cell phone in his hand.

I finally say what I met with Grady to say. "The way I see it, we can spend a ton of time trying to find Tom and likely be no further ahead."

"Or?"

"Or we can give the police some options."

"How so?" Grady says, dropping the cell phone and looking at me. He has a gleam in his eyes. A little sparkle in the corners.

"You don't believe Tom had anything to do with Ben's disappearance, do you?"

"Not a chance," Grady says. "Absolutely no way."

"Then we need to figure out who could have."

Grady nods, staring out the window. "So where do we start?"

"I've been thinking about this," I say. "Detective Evans told me there are three main reasons kids disappear. One, they take off. But that doesn't seem like something Ben would do. Another is that someone has snatched them. Which we can't rule out. I mean, it's possible. I never noticed anyone watching Ben, but that doesn't mean there wasn't. It would be awful, and I don't even want to think about it. So..."

"What is the third way?"

"Family," I say. "That's number one."

Grady smiles. "The Carters," he says.

"The Carters," I say.

"You want to dig into the mayor's life?"

"And of his kids."

"What about Erin?"

"Erin as well," I say.

"I don't know if I want to start digging into the mayor's life," Grady says.

"Right now I bet Detective Evans isn't even considering looking at the mayor or his family. She's only got eyes for Tom. We have to give her options."

"This is not the kind of trouble I'm looking for," Grady says.

"What did you say before about not getting caught?"

"I don't get caught because I don't do stupid things like investigating public officials."

"They have their secrets, Grady. You know they do. I mean, who doesn't?"

Grady laughs. "Yeah, who doesn't?"

"Right now the police are focused on Tom. What if something else is going on? Detective Evans would never even know. We have to do this for Tom."

"For Tom," Grady says. He rubs the steering wheel. "This could be really dangerous."

"What, you want a nice ordinary life? You going to go code the next *Angry Birds* or something?"

"That's exactly my plan. How'd you know?" he says. "I guess I'll have to put that on hold."

"So you're in?"

"For Tom," he says. "But we have to be careful."

"I'm always careful," I say.

Grady looks at me with a healthy dose of eyebrow-raised skepticism.

"What's Tom been telling you about me?" I say.

"Nothing," Grady says. "Nothing at all."

SIXTEEN

It is down to one police car outside the Carters' house. We drive a block away, and Grady edges in and parks behind a minivan in the shadow of a large maple. He pulls a laptop from the backseat.

"What are you doing?" I ask.

"Seeing who has open Wi-Fi connections around here." He is typing and flicking his index finger madly across the trackpad. He pauses for a moment and turns the stereo on. Horns fill the car's interior.

"What's this?" I say.

"Otis Redding," Grady replies. "'Pain in My Heart.'" He looks at me. "I need music to work."

"And what's the work we're doing here?" I say, looking at the middle-class homes around us.

"The work of finding out what the Carters have to hide," he says. "And look here, there's a network going by the name of Carters Corner. Isn't that sweet?"

"Can you connect to it?" I lean over and look at the screen, my shoulder pressed tightly against Grady's.

"I should be able to in a second. A lot of people never change the default security setting. A couple of months ago, this hacking group managed to shut down a broadcast of the president's State of the Union address because the TV station hadn't ever changed a router from its default user name and password." He opens a new window on the screen. "The router is like a door into a house. People feel that having a password on their computers is inconvenient, or they don't have anything worth stealing. Yet here we are, half a block from the Carters' house, and their entire digital lives are available to us." He looks at me as people do when you've just told them you believe in giant salamanders ruling the world. "I mean, you wouldn't go out and leave your doors open, would you? And if you did, if you left your door open and someone walked in, they would steal your things. A TV, microwave maybe, jewelry. Leave your Wi-Fi open, and you're letting people steal your thoughts, your passwords, your entire digital being."

"I lock everything down," I say, almost defensively.

"People are getting better, for sure. But you only have to let your guard down for a minute."

"You're scary," I say.

"Hey, you're the one asking me to do this," Grady says. He pushes a finger against the laptop screen. "It looks like they have a number of computers connected. And only one has a password. It might also be a police laptop."

"You mean by the computer's name?"

"Yeah, it's called Mobile Unit 822. That doesn't sound like the name of a personal computer."

"That's Detective Evans—822 is the number she kept saying when she called in," I say. "Everything was *822 responding* or *822 en route.*"

Grady looks up from the laptop screen. "Tell me about Detective Evans," he says.

"Like what?"

"Is she married?"

"Yeah," I say. "She has two kids, a girl and a boy. She's really only a step away from the picket-fence-and-fresh-baked-cookie crowd."

"Do you know their names?"

I think back to my conversation with Detective Evans on Sunday morning. "Paul and Emma."

"Good." Grady types something. "What else?"

"Um, she went to school here."

"Which school?"

"Leslie, I think. She said something about living in that part of town."

"Okay." He types some more. "What else? How old is she?"

"I don't know."

He moves his finger around on the trackpad. "Thirty-eight," he says. "How old are her kids?"

"Ten and twelve. How do you know how old she is?"

"There's an article here from when she made detective. A local-paper thing. What else do you know?"

I think, but nothing comes. "Nothing, I guess."

Grady is typing away. I close my eyes and breathe in the fresh spring air.

"56 Legacy Avenue," he says.

"What's that?" I ask without opening my eyes.

"Her address. It's under her husband's name. Andrew Richler. She didn't take his last name." Grady is silent for a moment. The only sounds are the tapping of his fingers on the keys and birds calling to one another from the nearby trees.

"Ah, there we are," he says. "Got it."

"Got what?"

"Into her computer."

I open my eyes and lean against his shoulder again. The desktop screen has changed. The wallpaper is now the police-force logo, and the cursor is moving around on its own.

"See, this is what I'm saying about hacking. I've never been interested in it. It's way too creepy."

"Her password is her dog's name, Barney, and her house address, 56. Eight characters. One capital, two numbers. Pretty basic. You'd think a police officer would create something a little more elaborate." Grady points at a program running near the bottom of his screen. "As for the hacking part, that's not entirely what happened. I put all the information I had on Detective Evans into this program, and it kept trying passwords until it got the right one."

"How did you know her dog's name?"

Grady enlarges the screen. "Another newspaper article. Barney's a rescue dog. Apparently he saved someone from a burning building. And then Detective Evans saved him from the needle."

"Good for Barney."

Grady laughs and points at a little map on the screen with a blinking symbol on it. "And there is your phone," he says.

"So she *is* the one tracking me."

Grady starts typing again. "I'll download everything I can from her computer. She has all her case files on here. We can find out if they have any other suspects."

"What does it say about Tom?" I lean against him again. This time, I think I feel him leaning back.

"I haven't opened any of the documents. We'll grab everything first, then go over it later."

"This can't be legal," I say.

Grady tilts a hand back and forth before him. "It's a gray area. She's on an unprotected network, so that's her bad. I did use a program to get into her computer, but not directly. I didn't *hack* it. I just needed some technological help to figure out her password."

"So you're saying what we're doing here is fine?"

"Yeah, pretty much a gray area."

"Probably not legal," I say.

"Gray. But anyway, you'd have to get caught before any of these things would matter. And, like I said, I don't get caught..."

"But in seventh grade you..."

"Anymore."

I let that go as Grady becomes more engrossed in the documents on his laptop. At first he reads bits out to me, but after a while he moves on to muttering to himself and shaking his head. The song changes. I actually recognize it. Sam Cooke, "Bring It On Home to Me."

"What do you think of Tom?" I ask. I figure he can easily read and talk to me at the same time. He seems the multi-tasking type.

"What do you mean?" Grady says, not looking up.

"Like, as a person."

"I think he's awesome."

"Why?"

"Why?"

"Yeah, why?" Grady doesn't say anything, so I fill the silence. "I've known him all my life. He's always just been there, you know? So I guess I'm not the best judge of his character anymore. Detective Evans told me to stand back from my relationship with Tom and really think about what I know. But you know him in ways I don't. So what you know is kind of like standing back."

"He's awesome because he is what he is," Grady says. "He never pretends to be anyone. He has no concept of what other people think of him at all. It's complete social blindness. There's every possibility that in his head he's worrying over what people are thinking about him or saying, but I don't see it."

"He's always been like that," I say.

"And he is really kind. I don't know that many kind people."

"No?"

"My mom's all right, but she gets really petty about a lot of things. She worries what people are doing and saying and thinks that everyone is out to screw her over. My uncle is cool too, but he rips people off whenever he sees the opportunity. Tom is Tom. He's never asked me for anything or talked badly about anyone. I sometimes tear into different bands because they suck or have sold out or were talentless fame whores to begin with, and somehow he always sees something good in their music. Some little turn or twist. Something honest."

"He's like that with everyone. Even my dad."

"What's wrong with your dad?" Grady asks.

"He tried to use us to punish our mother," I admit. "I'm not sure if he knew he was doing it, but it happened. He fought for custody for the longest time. Tom eventually gave himself up. He convinced our dad that it would be best if he lived with him and I stayed with Mom. I think our dad was a little freaked at the idea of raising me. Like, he wouldn't know what to do with a girl in the house. Tom moved across town with him, and we didn't see one another that much.

Like, on weekends and stuff, but never for long. My dad likes to drink too much and tell people what he thinks. I imagine Tom took a lot of his anger."

"He lives with you now, right?"

"My dad met someone and moved to California. Tom moved back in with us, but he stayed at Mitchell Mayer to finish school. My dad's new wife, or whatever she is, has two boys. The type of boys my dad likely always wanted. Football playing, girl hunting, upwardly mobile."

"Good riddance then?" Grady says cautiously.

"Yes, for sure. We don't need him in our lives."

"You always have to be careful when it comes to people's families," Grady says. "I mean, you can talk about how awful a person is, how he's a prick and an alcoholic and a total dirtbag, but that's only because that alcoholic dirtbag is your father. Someone else says a cruel word about the guy, and it's war."

"It's not war," I say. "I'm likely eternally damaged by his lack of interest. But right now I'm just happy he's gone."

"I've never sensed that Tom is seriously damaged or anything. He never says a bad word about anyone, ever."

"He really likes Ben as well," I say. "That's for certain. Tom actually hung out with us a lot when I was babysitting."

"Did you tell the police that?"

"No," I say. "It would look bad, don't you think?"

"Absolutely. But then, if they ever discover that, it's not going to look good on you." Grady points at his laptop screen. "So Tom is definitely suspect number one."

"Not a surprise," I say. Though it still makes me angry to hear it.

"It has been decided that the parents couldn't have had anything to do with it."

"Why?" I ask, leaning over to look at the screen.

"Detective Evans writes here, *I'm confident this is not a case of parental abduction.* But seriously, both of them are there, right? So how could it be?"

"Is there anyone else?" I ask. Grady scrolls down the page. "What's that?"

"That's Jack's computer," Grady says. "It's connected to the network, so it shows up."

"We should look through that," I say. "Who knows what's in there."

"Good idea," Grady says. He drags the folder onto his own browser window.

As we watch the files move, I say, "Detective Evans told me it was most likely family."

"She did?" Grady says.

"She wasn't talking about this case. Just in general. When kids that age disappear, it almost always has a family connection."

"There's nothing here," Grady says. "As far as I can see, they don't have a clue."

"Except Tom," I say.

"Except Tom," Grady replies.

SEVENTEEN

"We need to get you back to your phone before someone gets suspicious," Grady says as he starts the car.

I shift in my seat, slip out of my shoes and put my feet on the dash. We roll through town, taking the long way back to the coffee shop. I stay quiet, for the most part, looking out the window and listening to the procession of soul music. Grady's arm twitches whenever he moves the steering wheel, causing the tattoos he has along his forearm to become more 3-D. I glance at him whenever I think his attention is totally elsewhere. He's clenching his jaw and appears to be deep in thought. As we drive past an empty cruiser parked outside the Starbucks, I say, "Do you think it will look suspicious?"

"What?" Grady says.

"How long I've apparently been sitting in a Starbucks."

As he pulls into the alley, Grady grabs a different laptop from the backseat. "Here, take this. If anyone asks, you're working on a young-adult novel. Tell them it's about vampires and zombies."

"I can't take your computer," I say.

"This one doesn't work."

"Won't that look even more suspicious? Me working away on a nonfunctioning computer?"

"Keep it closed. It'll seem as if you're contemplating what the love child of a vampire and a zombie would look like. You know, trying to figure out that exact phrase to perfectly summarize the beast."

I'm about to get out when I think of something. "What does it say in the report about Steph and JJ?"

"I didn't see much. Just that JJ and Steph were both at their mother's home on the night in question. No reason to suspect they were anywhere else. To all appearances they love their stepbrother and miss him. That's it. But why *would* either of them snatch their brother? What could possibly be gained?"

"Oh, I don't know. To get back at their dad. Because they hate their stepmom. Because JJ wants a new car or Steph wants more jewelry and ho boots."

"Not a fan of the Carter kids, I see," Grady says.

"They are not my favorite people. No."

"But do you think they could have anything to do with Ben's disappearance?"

"I don't know," I say. "I can't think of any reason why."

"We need a why," Grady says. "If we're going to get the police off Tom's back, we need as many whys as possible."

"They weren't at their mother's house all night, and if that's what it says in the report, someone's been lying. They were at the same beach party I was. I told Detective Evans that on Sunday."

"You go to beach parties?" Grady says.

"It happens," I say. "I prefer the pool party. You know, hot tubs and all." I open the door. Grady gives me a raised eyebrow. "People go to parties," I say, leaning back in. "The Carter kids were there most of the night, as far as I remember."

"Okay. Sure. The next time they're at their parents' place, I'll put a little gift on their phones," Grady says. "Then we can see what they're texting and viewing and where they are."

"*That* sounds illegal."

He rotates his hand in front of himself.

"I know, I know," I say, before he can. "It's a gray area."

"Gray. Exactly. How about I pick you up tonight around seven, and we'll swing by the Carters' place again and see who's there. Plus, I only managed to download about half of the files on the mayor's computer. I'd like to grab the rest, if I can."

"Okay. Sure. Thanks for this, Grady."

"I'd be doing it anyway," Grady replies. "But it's nice to have company."

－－－－－

The first person I see upon reentering Starbucks is Detective Evans. She's seated by the front window. There's a coffee on the table in front of her. At first I think I might be able to sneak to the counter and retrieve my phone from the barista without being seen, but Detective Evans spots me the second I emerge from the hallway. She waves me over. I edge past a couple of people to stand beside the table.

"Lauren," she says, without a hint of surprise in her voice. "Shouldn't you be in school?"

"I took a mental-health day."

"Oh, are you not feeling well?" Someone brushes against me. Detective Evans shifts the other chair out from her table. "Do you want to sit down?"

"No, actually I just came in here to get my phone. I forgot it earlier."

"Give me two minutes," Detective Evans says. I want to ask her what she is doing here, but I already know. She followed me here and came in to question me some more. I decide, at least initially, to play the frightened-of-the-police little girl. I put Grady's laptop on the table. Detective Evans looks at it, then back at me. I sit down, my back to the restaurant, the hard sun streaming straight into my eyes.

"That brick through your window scared you a bit, didn't it?" She's gone all soft-voiced, which is totally not her style.

"Not really," I say.

"No?"

"It was likely some idiot who believes everything he hears on the news. You know, all the official statements."

Detective Evans sips at her coffee. "No one has ever said that your brother has anything to do with Benjamin's disappearance."

"It's assumed."

"I don't have control over what the media puts out, Lauren," Detective Evans says.

"Do you have any other suspects?"

"Your brother is not a suspect." She has a stony look on her face. As if she had to erase all emotions in order to make the statement.

"Really?"

"We need to talk to him," she says. "Have you heard from him?"

"No."

"Are you sure?"

It's getting hot sitting in the sun. "I said I haven't."

"Hmmm." Detective Evans taps the top of her coffee cup. "The truth shall set you free, Lauren. Have you heard that?"

I close my eyes to the sun. It's really intense. Plus a Miley Cyrus song is playing, and the two things combined, intense sun and horrible lyrics, are giving me a headache. "Sure."

"You'll feel so much better if you simply tell us everything you know. I do believe that."

I lean back out of the sun. "Which truth?" I ask.

"*The* truth," Detective Evans says, nodding in agreement with herself.

"But what is that? Ben is missing. That's the truth. My brother has nothing to do with it. That's the truth as well. But you don't see it that way."

"He may not have anything to do with Benjamin's disappearance, Lauren. That is a possible truth. But we still need to speak to him. There's no debating the fact that he was seen in the area that night."

"What about that rumor about him and the kid in the park?"

"Lauren, I told you—"

I interrupt her. "What was the truth that time? Tom was playing with a kid, and an overprotective mother decided he was '*being weird.*' People got freaked out and made up all kinds of stories, and now Tom's a weirdo. Period. That's the truth for so many people. And if he's bothered one kid before, then of course…"

"That was one event, Lauren. We don't take that as the complete story."

"So stop splashing his picture on the TV beside Benny's," I say. "Put an end to the rumor."

"I don't have control over that, Lauren."

I feel as if I'm talking to a recording. Detective Evans is going to keep saying the same thing over and over. She isn't allowed to step outside of this official message. Miley Cyrus changes to a Decemberists song.

"So," she says. "Do you have any idea where Tom might be?"

"I don't," I say. I feel like screaming at her. But what good would that do?

"Okay, Lauren," Detective Evans says. "Okay."

"I have to go," I say. "My mother is still freaked out."

"Of course," Detective Evans says. "You go home and take care of your family. Be safe."

And I don't know if that's a suggestion or a threat.

EIGHTEEN

We find a parking spot beneath a broken streetlight a few car lengths away from where we parked earlier. I slouch down in my seat as the engine ticks to silence.

"Are we close enough to connect to their Wi-Fi?" I ask. Grady has his laptop propped up on his knees. The radio is tuned to a quiet jazz station. Every so often an announcer comes on and, in low tones, talks about what we are about to hear.

"We should be."

"I saw Steph's car out front when we passed."

"Well, let's see if her phone's connected." He types on the keyboard while I stare into the darkness. He's still wearing a white shirt and tie, though he's changed into 501s and a pair of gray Etnies. "Is your cell on?"

"No. I have it with me, but I left it off. I had a feeling we didn't need anyone following us right now."

"Good," Grady says. "I made sure they can't track your calls or texts, by the way."

"That's good to know." I sit up and look out at the dark street.

"Ah, there we go, I'm in." Grady turns the screen toward me. "The cool thing about this program is that you can see what the person is doing on their phone in real time."

"So this is Steph's phone?" I ask.

"It is. It looks like she's searching the Internet for information about the upcoming *America's Next Top Model* episode and texting some guy named Justin."

"This is awesome and everything," I say, "but also really creepy."

Grady shrugs. "They could actually use passwords. That's all it takes."

"But if they had passwords, you would hack them anyway, right?"

"Not necessarily."

"But probably," I say.

Grady turns back to the computer. "You'd think someone so heartbroken by the disappearance of her sweet little baby brother would be less interested in which scary-thin woman is going to be expelled from a reality show. Wouldn't you?"

"You obviously don't know Steph Carter," I say.

"That is seriously shallow."

I watch as a line of characters cuts across her texting screen. "What did she just type?"

"*Eight is better*," Grady says. "I guess she's meeting someone."

I say, "That's her boyfriend, Justin Prince."

Grady closes his eyes and turns his face toward the ceiling. "Prince, Prince. Where do I know that name from? Is he related to Doug Prince?"

"Brothers," I say.

"Again, your enthusiasm for others is immense. What have the Prince brothers done to impress you so?" Grady pushes his sleeve up. He's wearing a studded bracelet and a few rings. I wonder if he decided to get dressed up for the evening.

"Do you know Doug Prince?" I ask.

"I know *of* Doug. One-time star quarterback, sky-high SATs. I believe he's been tirelessly working on a cure for cancer since graduation."

"That's the one."

"So I've heard of Justin as well. And he is most definitely not curing cancer. I believe he is beloved in our fair city as the bringer of the magical weed. The guy who moves major product." He's typing on the laptop again. "Does Justin look like his brother?"

"A little," I say. "His hair's longer, and he's got some tats."

"Neither of these things make him evil," Grady says. With his sleeves rolled up, I can see the many tattoos covering his arms. They look to be linked sets. A seascape on one arm, some kind of an underworld scene on the other.

"I wasn't saying that."

"It's what's in his dark, dark heart that makes him evil," Grady says. He reads something off the screen. "I was right. Justin Prince is a middleman. He gets the product into the city, then distributes it to dealers who dime-bag it."

"And where did you get such classified information?"

"A friend of a friend knows a guy whose cousin—"

"Okay, okay. What does this have to do with us?" I ask.

"Well, you'd think the police would be interested in a little lost boy's stepsister being so close to a drug kingpin."

"You'd call him a kingpin?" I say.

"Work with me here. If we're looking to divert attention from Tom and maybe get people thinking differently, then, possibly, the police would be interested in how Steph spends her idle hours."

"And with who," I say.

"I believe that would be whom," Grady says as he starts the engine.

"You're the grammar police now as well?"

"It's whom, not who. That's all. I'm no kind of police at all."

"Where are we going?" I say.

"Steph is leaving," Grady says. "We need to follow her."

With the laptop still balanced on one leg, Grady stops at the corner and glances up the street.

"She insisted Justin meet her. His reply was that he had something to take care of first. To which Stephanie replied, *I'm coming with you. You promised.*" Grady looks at me. "I've never met her, and I can almost hear her voice."

"It's whiny, for sure, but more of a *tired of everything slash the world and its problems are all beneath me.*"

"Complicated."

"Not so much."

"Anyway, Justin has given in and Stephanie should be en route to meet him at an as-yet-undisclosed location."

"Do you think it's for a drug deal?" Headlights flash across the street as Steph's Jetta swings out of the driveway.

"I don't know. We might get lucky. It looks like your Detective Evans is staying at the Carters' place." I squint into the darkness but can't see any cars in the Carters' driveway. "Or, at least, her computer is." Grady hands me the laptop. "Keep an eye on that screen. I get the feeling Steph might be a distracted driver." Steph pulls up to the intersection in front of us and stops. When she pulls away, Grady turns his headlights back on and drives away from the curb.

"You'll still be able to see what she's texting even when not connected to their Wi-Fi?"

"Yeah, all her texts are relayed through the Internet now. I have a 4G connection on that laptop, so we shouldn't lose her."

"That's awesome," I say. "Way better to look at this screen than my phone." Grady nods, already seemingly lost in thought. Soon enough it's just the ping of a light rain across the windshield and the tires humming over pavement. Grady flips on the windshield wipers as we follow Steph into the downtown core. I turn the brightness of the screen down and tilt the laptop so my face isn't lit up by it.

"She texts a lot while driving," I say.

"She's all over the road," Grady says. "I'm surprised she hasn't hit anyone."

"It's like a talent."

"But not really," Grady says. "Or else she'd be doing a halfway decent job at it. What has she written?"

"Sulky stuff about wanting to be included in his life. Not just some bitch on his arm. Something about possibly being an asset. Justin has yet to reply to any of this, by the way." I watch the screen. Another text pops up. "You're kidding me."

"What?"

"They're meeting at the Denny's."

"What?" Grady laughs. "That's depressing. I'm not into the whole drug-culture-is-cool thing, but holy crap. *Denny's?*"

"Maybe they're meeting there before going to some decrepit, dirty place to do the deal."

"Can you imagine handing a bunch of weed across a table at Denny's? Having to move the little maple-syrup holder? 'Hey, can someone hold this ketchup? There's a lot of product here.'"

Steph pulls into the Denny's parking lot. We drive on past and turn in to the adjoining strip mall's lot. "Looks like he's just picking her up," I say.

"My faith in the counterculture remains." Less than a minute later, a large Jeep parks beside Steph's Jetta. Steph hops out and slips into the passenger seat.

"We'll need to be a little more careful now," Grady says. "I don't know Justin personally, but I suspect he will be more suspicious than Miss Carter."

"And by suspicious you mean paranoid," I say.

"Exactly."

We wait to see which way Justin turns, let a couple of cars pass, then pull out.

"We should be able to follow him at a distance no problem," Grady says. "As long as we make all the same lights." We tail the Jeep through town and out onto the highway. Grady slips in behind a minivan and stays there as the Jeep gains speed. The high and heavy streetlights have flashed on along the median. It will be like this for another couple of miles, and then there will be nothing but head-lights cutting through the rain-drenched dusk.

This is my favorite time of day to travel. The dimness, along with the thundering of the wheels over pavement, makes me feel as if I could be anywhere.

"There are only two exits along here," Grady says. The rain has picked up, and he has the windshield wipers going full blast. His jaw is locked again, and he's staring intensely out the window. "I think I might know where they're going."

"Where?" I say.

"If my friend is right, Justin gets his product from a biker gang. And there happens to be a biker bar out here. Keep looking to your side. The exit is coming up."

A moment later, the Jeep signals and pulls off.

"They're taking the turnoff," I say as Grady blows past the exit. "Where are you going?"

"I have an idea."

"Please share," I say, grabbing the dash and holding on for dear life.

"Turn your phone on. Hopefully, someone will follow us." Grady swerves back and forth around traffic and turns onto an access road.

"How does Justin dress?" he asks.

"Polo shirts and chinos. Why?"

"Hand-me-downs from his brother?"

"I doubt it."

"How do you think that particular look would go over in a bar filled with leather-clad bikers?"

"Not well at all."

"And what with Justin being only seventeen, I imagine this exchange will be in the parking lot. With this rain, it'll happen really fast."

"Would you like to fill me in on what exactly you are doing?" There are no lights along the access road. Nor are there any cars. Just a few houses and open fields. Grady suddenly pulls off the road and into a driveway, shutting down the headlights as we come to a stop.

"I'm trying to give the police some options. Or, at the very least, some questions. Here, hand me the laptop." Grady grabs the laptop before I have a chance to move. "Okay. One second."

I roll down my window, and the thumping bass of "Sweet Home Alabama" flows into the car. The wind has died down, leaving the rain to fall straight down. "That's loud," I say.

"The bar is right next door." Headlights appear along the access road. "That has to be a cruiser," Grady says. "Quick, turn off your cell."

I hold the power button down, and the screen goes dark. "It's off."

"Yes, I think that worked."

"What?" I say. I have absolutely no idea what is going on.

"The police locater is locked to Steph's phone. Now we have to hope the police have some reason to pull Justin over."

"Why would they do that?" I ask.

Grady reaches into the backseat as a cruiser passes and slows. It pulls off onto the shoulder. "Are you telling me that a cop was sent out to follow me the second my cell came on?"

"Someone noticed you heading out of town, I guess. If they believe you have contact with Tom, they'd be curious as to where you were going."

I nod.

"Go, Mr. Policeman," he says, waving his hands at the cruiser. "They're going to drive away."

The cruiser stays put. It's not hidden at all.

Grady grabs a cell phone from the backseat. "Come on," he says. He looks at the phone. The cruiser remains, a light bubbling of raindrops on its roof. "We're going to have to give them a reason to pull Justin over," he says. He dials a number, then holds the phone to his ear. "Hello…yes, my vehicle was struck by a black Jeep thingie along Ridgeline Road," Grady says in a ridiculously high voice. "I have the license number, if that would help. I don't want to confront the driver though. It happened outside the Ridgeline Roadhouse, and, well, you know the type of people who…Sorry, what?…Oh, of course." He reads out a license-plate number. "Oh, wait, I think I might see it. I don't think they meant to do it. It's just this rain. It's…Yes, I can hold." He closes the phone, then opens it again and snaps it in two.

"Who were you supposed to be?" I say.

"That's my little old lady," Grady says. "I also have an older British gentleman and a southern dude who spits a lot." He grins. "Okay now. Wait for it, wait for it…"

The cruiser, which has been parked no more than fifty feet from us, suddenly pulls onto the road and takes off with lights flashing.

"I have a feeling that Justin Prince's dealing days are, for the time being, over."

"They won't really have a reason to search the car, will they?" I say.

"It all depends on how well the pot is wrapped. Let's hope Justin decided to test the wares prior to purchase." Grady starts the car and pulls to the end of the driveway. A pack of bikers flashes past. The roar of their big engines is deafening.

"Bizarre that a group of bikers would suddenly take off in the rain, isn't it?" Grady says. "Think how wet they're going to be."

We follow them away from the roadhouse. I watch in the side mirror as Justin gets out of the car with his hands in the air.

"Hit that Disconnect button on the screen," Grady says.

"What will that do?" I ask as I click the button.

"Turn your cell back on," Grady says. He giggles. Actually giggles. It makes me laugh in return.

"Okay," I say, trying to stem the flow of my own laughter. I turn my cell back on. "What are we laughing about?"

"How easy this is," Grady says.

"Aren't the police going to figure out that I know they're tracking me?"

"Oh, absolutely," Grady says, taking a few breaths to slow his giggles. "But they sure aren't going to say anything."

He looks over at me. I cover my mouth, but it's impossible to hold it in.

We return to our laughing fits, bowled over in the moment at having actually, somehow, accomplished something.

NINETEEN

WEDNESDAY

I know Grady was right the second I see Detective Evans leaning against the window in Principal Smith's office the next morning.

"My presence was requested?" I say. I've been pulled out of History class.

Principal Smith stands. "Lauren, I believe you know Detective Evans?" I don't respond, so the principal goes on. "She would like a word with you. She has requested that it simply be the two of you, but school policy requires me to be in attendance unless…"

"It's okay with me," I say. "I'm sure Detective Evans just has a few quick questions. Right? Or maybe an update on the investigation into who they think threw that brick through our window."

"A couple of questions, Lauren," Detective Evans says. She turns and leans against a table beneath the window. "It shouldn't take more than a few minutes."

"Okay," Principal Smith says, skirting around her desk. "I'll leave you to it." She exits the office, closing the door behind her, and for the first time since meeting Detective Evans, I don't feel intimidated. She has her arms crossed and is looking down at me. I stand a little straighter.

"How are you today, Lauren?" Detective Evans asks.

"All right," I respond. I hold my hands behind my back and put a foot against the wall. "I think I can get through the day. My mom is still pretty freaked out."

"Can I ask where you were last night, Lauren?" Detective Evans says.

"Mostly at home. Why?"

"Any word from your brother yet?"

"No."

Detective Evans pushes away from the table and walks behind Principal Smith's desk. "Have you heard what happened with Stephanie Carter?"

I pause, as though I might not answer. I give her a big shrug. "Rumors."

"Such as?" Detective Evans says.

"Something about how Steph and her boyfriend were busted with a very large amount of marijuana. But that's nothing more than a rumor, right?" I make certain to open my eyes wide and blink.

"I can't verify anything at the moment," Detective Evans says. I feel a little laugh bubble up inside me but manage to push it back down. "Have you ever visited the Ridgeline Roadhouse?"

"Where's that?" I ask, hopefully looking confused.

"Ridgeline Road."

I give my head a quick shake and say, "That's outside of town, right? I don't drive. We don't even have a car."

"So you had no idea that Stephanie Carter was at the Roadhouse last night?"

"Why would I?" I say. It's tiring, putting out half-truths all the time. I have discovered that answering questions with questions works pretty well.

I pull my cell phone out of my pocket, glance at it as if it's buzzed, then slip it back in.

"Lauren, where were you last night?"

I shake my head as if the whole situation is baffling. She knows I know she knows. I almost giggle at the sound of that thought. *She* knows *I* know *she* knows.

But she can't admit to putting the app on my phone. That would be illegal. She also, as far as I know, has no real reason to formally interview me.

Which allows me to go on the offensive.

"I didn't know that I had to explain my every move to the local police force," I say. "Am I suspected of something? Or is this what happens to people now?"

"You are not suspected of anything, Lauren."

"Then why so much interest? Did you find out who threw a brick through our window?"

"We're still investigating," Detective Evans says.

I give her a slow nod. "Because, like I said, it has my mother terrified. What if we'd been sitting in the living room?"

"There's not much we can do about it, Lauren. The footprints can give us a general idea of sex, size and weight, but that's about it."

"And what size, weight and sex have you discovered the person is?"

"I can't discuss that."

"Of course you can't. And what about Ben? Do you have any leads there?"

"You know that's why we need to talk to your brother." She's been pushing a thumb against her cuticles. She suddenly laces her hands and cracks her fingers.

"Because he's not a suspect or anything," I say.

Detective Evans smiles, giving her neck a quick tweak. "Because we need to talk to—"

"Because if the rumors about Steph are true," I interrupt, "then I have to wonder if maybe you're looking in the wrong places."

"How so?"

"Well, if Stephanie Carter is dealing drugs, wouldn't it be possible that someone grabbed Ben for revenge or a missed payment or something?"

"I highly doubt that happens outside of movies," Detective Evans says, a patronizing little smile on her face as if I'm a child who is asking a silly question. "And at the moment, we don't know—"

"But how can you be sure?" I say. "I mean, if you had no idea that Stephanie was into this kind of thing until last night—which I have to assume is true or else she would have been arrested ages ago, right?—what else don't you know about her? Maybe she sold Ben to buy more drugs."

"You're being ridiculous," Detective Evans says.

I shrug. "Oh. Okay. I see." I push off the wall and move across the room to the desk. I sit on the arm of one of the two chairs there. "What was it you were saying about the truth before? That it will set me free? What is the truth now? Because it seems to me it has changed."

"Nothing has changed, Lauren. We still need to talk to your brother. If you know where he is and aren't telling us, then you can be charged with—"

"Even though he's not a suspect or anything," I interrupt again.

"Even though he might not be a suspect."

"Might not be." I nod in agreement. "Okay, gotcha. Can I go now? I'm missing History." Detective Evans narrows her eyes at me.

"Good luck with that whole Stephanie Carter thing," I say. "Can we expect to see her picture up beside Ben's now as well? If the rumors are true, that was a lot of marijuana she was found with. It really feels like a thing you'd normally see on the evening news. So there'll be a report, right? All the media outlets have been alerted? We'll see bags of pot laid out for the cameras, street values being estimated for the general public, all that?" I stare at Detective Evans for another moment. She stares back. "Yeah, I didn't think so." I open the office door and step out.

In the hallway, I close my eyes and take a few deep breaths before walking away.

— — — —

I decide not to return to class. I'm too angry to pay attention. Besides, I may as well use the fact that everyone is tiptoeing around me to my advantage.

Instead, I text Grady to meet me at the Starbucks. Then I shut my phone down.

I know I've thrown out a red flag for Detective Evans. If she ever saw me as an innocent, frightened teenager, she no longer does.

She knows I'm capable of lying to her. If anything, I'm going to be followed that much more closely now.

I'm almost out the door when JJ Carter steps out of a hallway and blocks my way.

"What did you do?" he says.

The hallway is empty but for us. Everyone is in class. JJ's face is all red.

"What are you talking about, JJ?" I say.

"Why was Detective Evans talking with you?" He gets closer to me. His arms are back, his chest out. I remember him in third grade, endlessly being reprimanded by Mr. Gordon for picking his nose. Once, Mr. Gordon turned JJ's desk over to show the class his booger collection. He was humiliated. I hold on to this image as the stink of Axe body spray assaults me.

"She was just following up on some information I gave her."

JJ gets scary close. "About Steph?"

"What about Steph?" I say, deciding to play dumb.

He screws up his face at me. "Your brother took my brother," JJ says, getting even closer. "I don't know why, but I know he did it."

"He didn't," I say. "Why would he?"

"Because he's a pervert. That's why. Your whole family is messed up." I back away, and he grabs my arm. "Where is he? Where is your brother? I swear to God, I'll rip your throat out if you don't tell me."

"Mr. Carter!"

JJ lets go of me as our History teacher, Mr. King, runs toward us.

"What are you doing?"

"Nothing," JJ replies.

"Are you all right, Lauren?" I love Mr. King a little right then. Love him in his vest and tie. Love him with his long hair and tattoos.

"Sure," I say, rubbing my arm.

"What was going on here?"

I back away. JJ is still glaring at me. I keep thinking *booger-boy* because that's how JJ was known for years, and I almost laugh.

"I have to go," I say.

"Lauren, come back," Mr. King says.

But I start running.

I saw something in JJ's eyes I didn't like. A real and true hatred.

— — — —

The Starbucks is empty. It's almost noon, and the lunch crowds have filled the restaurants along the street. The barista from the day before greets me and slides down the counter.

"Hiya," she says. "By the way, my name's Crystal." She extends a ring-covered hand.

"Lauren," I say.

"Are you meeting Grady again?"

"I am."

Crystal's eyes go all distant. I notice a butterfly tattoo on her neck. It seems to be pumping its wings. I look more closely and see that the body of the tattoo is right over the thick vein running up her neck.

"So did you two, like, date before or...?" I ask.

"I wish," she says. "It wouldn't have worked out, but it could have been fun for a while, right?"

"I don't know," I say.

Crystal leans back from the counter. She's wearing a tank top and a black vest above a pair of ripped jeans. She has a wealth of tattoos up her left arm but none on her right.

"Not to be rude, but you don't really seem his type," Crystal says.

"Oh, we're not dating."

"Why not? He's about the nicest guy I've ever met. He's smart. He doesn't buy into all the bullshit out there. He's, like, genuine."

"Okay, but I'm still not interested," I say.

"Yeah, keep that up. It'll drive him crazy. I came on too strong. But we've talked about it since, and it's obvious we wouldn't have worked. We're, like, too much the same. Listen, you want a coffee? I have an extra latte here."

"Sure," I say, wondering why there would be extra lattes anywhere. "Thank you." I've just sat down with my free drink when Grady comes in through the back door.

He looks around before sitting across from me. "Do you have your phone on?" he asks.

"No. I need you to take that program off now. That game is truly over."

"Did Detective Evans say something?" Grady asks, taking my phone.

"No, but she couldn't, could she?"

Crystal is suddenly at the table. She puts a tiny cup down in front of Grady. "Double espresso, I presume."

Grady smiles. "Thanks, Crystal." As she walks away, he downs the drink in one shot.

"She wanted to know what I was doing at the roadhouse last night," I tell him. "But since no one actually saw us there, she couldn't actually ask."

"And now that the signal is gone, she won't know where you are or what you're doing. It will drive her insane." He laughs, slides my phone across the table to me and looks out the window. "They can still track you if they want. But it'll have to be done legally. I can't see a judge giving her the right to tap your phone. You haven't done anything."

"I don't get why she doesn't believe me."

Grady shrugs. "Probably because you keep lying to her."

"Just now. I mean, with the Steph thing," I say to Grady's amusement.

"If she wasn't suspicious before, she really has reason to be now." His smile is genuine. He seems to be having a good time.

"Right after that, JJ Carter attacked me in the hallway."

"Attacked?" Grady says, looking worried.

"He grabbed me and told me how my family is messed up and how he would rip Tom's throat out. It was really scary."

"What a prick. Are you all right?"

"Yeah," I say, though I am not totally all right. "I'll be fine."

"Are you sure?" Grady is looking at me differently.

"The infuriating part is that they're still running Tom's picture with Ben's," I say. "I saw it on the news this morning."

"That must be coming from the mayor's office. I haven't seen anything about the drug bust either. If he asks for something to be kept quiet, it will be kept quiet."

"And JJ seems to know it."

"JJ is a different problem altogether." He's smiling again.

"Are you high?" I say.

"No, why?"

"You seem to be enjoying this too much."

"Well, everything but you getting attacked, yeah. That was never planned. But I like to think this way. We do something, then they do something, then it's our turn again. It's fun."

"Fun?"

"It would be if a kid wasn't missing and my best friend wasn't the main suspect and you didn't have a psychopath threatening you and throwing bricks through your window."

"Tom's your best friend?" I say.

Grady looks directly at me. "Somehow, it seems I get along well with your family. Which might give some credence to JJ's speculation that you're all a bit messed up."

"What about your uncle or people who work at the wrecker?"

"It's only my uncle and me, and I wouldn't call him a friend. Friends are people you choose to spend time with. You don't have a choice with your family."

"But you must have—" I begin before Grady interrupts.

"Are you trying to make me feel bad or something?"

"No, it's just…"

"I was homeschooled, remember? I spent mornings with my uncle, afternoons with my mom or alone. I've never been on a sports team. I moved between all these adults who hoped I'd turn out okay but didn't actually have a clue how to help that along. I worked at the record shop and had friends there, but that closed and they all moved on. Now I'm stuck with you and your brother."

"Stuck?" I say, trying to sound hurt.

"You just made a mockery of my life. You're not allowed to feel hurt." He smiles again, and it's really a very nice smile. He barely has to work at it.

"I'm not even certain who I am anymore," I say. Grady doesn't respond, so I go on. "Like today, when Detective Evans was grilling me, I didn't feel nervous at all."

"Good for you!"

"Okay, a little nervous. But, like, before I felt as if I'd done something wrong. Like I was a criminal or something. But that's not true. I haven't done anything wrong. And neither has Tom."

Grady leans back in his seat. "That's how the police operate. They need information, and people are vessels to get that information from. It's why this is all so much fun. It's a game for them, right? So…let's play the game." Grady crosses his arms and looks out the window. "It's, like, my dad.

Okay, he was drinking. He might have hit that guy. But no one really knows for certain. The police figured it was him. They had him on the side of the road and the timing all matched. But then they had to go and interview everyone around him. His family, friends, co-workers. They asked everyone about his drinking problem. He didn't have a drinking problem. He had a really bad day and decided to drink because of it. Stupid choice number one. He decided to drive home. Really stupid choice number two. But you ask about someone's drinking problem, and there's suddenly no debating it. That's the starting point. So instead of being able to say, 'He doesn't have a drinking problem,' you're forced to say, 'I didn't know he had a drinking problem,' and that's not fair. They ruined his life."

I drink some coffee and stay quiet. Grady goes on.

"He'll get out someday, but so what, right? What does it even matter anymore? His old life is gone. His co-workers think he's a lunatic. Which is why if you do talk to your brother, you need to get him to call Detective Evans."

"What? Why?" I say, caught totally unaware by this suggestion.

"Because he hasn't done anything. But the longer he's missing, the more likely it is they'll find something to pin on him."

"That's really paranoid," I say.

"The police were tracking you without your knowledge. You don't think they could find something to put on Tom to keep him in jail?"

"Isn't that all the more reason for him to stay missing? At least until Ben is found?"

"You mean *if* Ben is found," Grady says. Then he quickly adds, "Which he will be. For sure."

"I know."

"Yes," Grady says. "Absolutely." He taps the table, glances out the window. "I have some things to show you."

"What?" I say.

"They have to do with your friend JJ Carter."

"You have my attention," I say.

"It's a video on my laptop." He looks around the Starbucks. "This isn't really the place to watch it. Let's go to my uncle's shop."

"Okay," I say, grabbing my bag and standing up. "Let's go."

TWENTY

On the outside, Rodney's Wreckers looks like every other wrecking yard on the planet. Inside the main garage, though, it's a different situation altogether.

"This is incredibly clean," I say.

"That would be thanks to my uncle's OCD."

There are three cars and a couple of motorcycles in various states of repair. The floor is a pristine white. "There isn't even any oil on the ground," I say.

"Who wants to work in a giant mess? We leave that outside." Grady closes the door and walks to a desk on the far wall. Laptops blink from a bookshelf, neat and organized with all the outlets and cords linked through the back.

Grady sits at the desk and pulls a chair up beside him. "Grab a seat. I want to show you a couple of videos."

"Said the creepy guy to the young girl."

"Do you still find me creepy?" He looks right at me, his eyes narrowing.

"Depends on the videos, I guess." I get an eyebrow raise from him. He flicks on a monitor and opens a video player.

The image on the screen is of Erin and Jack sitting beside one another on the couch in their living room. A clock running in the bottom right corner of the screen shows that the video was made at eight thirty in the morning on the day Ben disappeared. Grady increases the volume.

The first voice I hear is Detective Evans. "And what time did you put Benjamin to bed last night?"

"Eight," Erin answers. "I gave him a bath, read him a story and tucked him in."

"Do you know if he went right to sleep?"

"Not likely. He never does. We normally get a half dozen visits from him after he's supposed to be asleep."

"What time did you last physically see him?"

"I went in at eleven thirty," Erin says, then looks to Jack, who shakes his head.

"I didn't go into his room last night. I was on the computer until midnight and then straight to bed." Jack Carter is wearing a dress shirt and perfectly creased pants, as if he'll be leaving for a business meeting at any moment.

"Do you remember when Jack came to bed?" Detective Evans asks, looking at Erin.

"Sure," Erin says. "It was right around midnight, like he said. I was still reading."

"So we know for certain that Benjamin was in bed at eleven thirty. Was he awake?"

"No," Erin says. "The second time I went in, he was out. I tucked him in again and gave him a kiss on the head and…" She stops and turns away from the camera. Jack glances at her but doesn't touch her. Not even a hand on her arm.

Nothing.

"I know this is difficult, but we need exact times so we can check security and red-light cameras. So the last time either of you saw Benjamin was at eleven thirty?"

Erin gives a slow nod. The camera shifts slightly, revealing JJ Carter sitting on a bar stool that has been placed behind the couch.

"When was the last time you saw Benjamin?" Detective Evans asks.

"Like, yesterday?" JJ says. He's wearing one of his trademark Abercrombie & Fitch polo shirts with professionally torn jeans. His hair is an oil spill. I think about how I looked when Detective Evans showed up at my place less than an hour after this interview. It wasn't pretty.

"Do you recall the time specifically?"

"Like, in the afternoon?"

"But not last night?"

"No." He shakes his head in an exaggerated motion.

"Did you sleep here last night?"

"No. At my place, like always. I'm here because I, like, need my dad's car this morning."

"What time did you arrive home?" Detective Evans asks.

"Oh, like, two?"

"Can I ask where you were?"

"Just at, like, a bonfire down on the beach."

Grady pauses the video. "This guy is awesome," he says.

"How?"

"Like, in every, like, way. Is he always, like, like that?"

"He's pretty hollow," I say. "If that's what you mean."

"Hollow. Yeah, that sounds right. I don't mean to judge here, but does he always look like a giant douche?"

"Pretty much."

"Look at that shirt! Eight o'clock on a Sunday morning, and he's flipped the collar as if he's being asked to stand in for a professional model. And that hair! Who does that?"

"The endlessly vain," I say.

Grady points at JJ on the monitor. "He doesn't seem all that concerned about his missing brother."

"Half brother," I say. "And yeah, you're right. It's like they're discussing where he might have left a skateboard."

Grady gets closer to the screen. "There's no emotion in his face."

"What do you mean?"

"When someone is upset or worried, their eyebrows go up and their forehead wrinkles. But there's none of that here. Also, he starts scratching his nose when he says he got home at two. And he's always looking away from Detective Evans."

"So?"

"That means he's probably lying."

"How do you know this stuff?" I say.

"I read a few books and watched a bunch of videos online about how you can tell if someone is lying."

"You can tell if someone is lying?"

"Don't freak out. It's not an automatic thing. You have to really focus. But in a situation like this, it's not very difficult. Why, have you been lying to me and I've missed it?"

"No," I say.

"Well, good," Grady says. "Nothing to worry about. Did you see what time JJ left the party?"

"I wasn't really watching him."

"Was this what he was wearing?"

I look at the video and realize I have no idea what JJ was wearing, even though I know I saw him at the party. "Not a clue."

"Detective Evans asks about you in a minute. Here." Grady starts the video, then fast-forwards.

"Did you see Lauren Saunders at this bonfire?"

"Yeah, like, for sure."

"Did you happen to notice when she left?"

"Why? You think she has something to do with this?"

"We're looking to follow up on everyone who came in contact with Benjamin over the past twenty-four hours. Lauren Saunders was with him yesterday."

"She was still there when I left," JJ says.

Grady pauses the video again and turns to me. "Were you?"

I look at the floor for a moment. "I don't know. I lost track of everything that night."

"Really? You don't remember when you left?"

This is not a conversation I want to be having with Grady. I mean, going to a party and drinking is one thing. Not having any idea what happened at that party is entirely another. Luckily, Grady restarts the video without another word. The camera swings to frame Erin and Jack again.

"Can you think of anyone, anyone at all, who might want to take Benjamin?" Detective Evans asks.

Jack immediately says no. Erin takes another second before saying, "No, no one."

Grady pauses the video. "So, she's lying there."

"What?" I say.

"I guess Detective Evans didn't pick up on it. But you can see it right here." Grady reverses the video slightly, leaving it paused. "Her eyes flick up and to the right."

"So what?" I say.

"Your eyes move in the direction you want to stimulate your brain. So if your eyes go up and to the left, you're stimulating the memory side of your brain. All your memories are stored in the left side. But if they go up and to the right, you're going for your imagination."

"So when Erin says she can't think of anyone, she's making up a story?"

"She's lying, I think. I mean, it's not a huge deal, but her eyes go up and to the right, and then she scratches her neck here." Grady advances the video again. "You get itchy when you lie. Because your adrenaline gets pumping when you're nervous, and your skin swells."

"So you think she knows of someone who would want to take Ben but isn't telling Detective Evans?"

"Possibly," Grady says, leaning back in his seat. "There are some things I'm looking at in Jack's financial statements. I don't have anything solid yet, but it feels as though there's someone out there no one knows about."

"What do you mean?" I say.

"I have to keep digging," he says. "I promise I'll let you in on it as soon as I find anything out. If there is anything to find out. Right now it's only a feeling."

"What's the other video?"

Grady pops forward in his seat. "Ah, yes, the walk-through."

"Walk-through of what?"

"The house."

On the screen is the Carters' hallway. "This is the main corridor to the bedrooms," Detective Evans's voice comes through the speakers. "The mother has informed us that the boy's door was closed. This is the room. We can see that the window remains open." The camera moves around the room as Detective Evans details the placement of the bed, the distance between various pieces of furniture, and how the scene does not appear to be one within which a struggle has taken place.

It is one of the most boring things I have ever sat through.

Grady pauses the video again. "Not only does there not seem to have been a struggle," he says, "but there's no evidence that anyone other than Ben was ever in the room."

"How can you tell that?"

Grady replays the last few seconds of the video. "See anything?"

"The window doesn't have a screen." I already knew this.

"Anything else?"

"No," I say.

"Exactly." He advances the video, laughing.

"You're enjoying this."

"It's pretty basic stuff. I mean, I've watched the whole video, and Detective Evans never says anything about this," Grady says, pointing at the screen. The video now shows the back-yard. A close-up of the house, with Ben's window in the center.

"What?"

"The garden," Grady says, nodding his head and pointing at it.

"What about it?"

"It's dirty."

I put my head in my hands. "That's kind of the point of a garden," I say.

"So if someone climbed in Ben's window, how come there's no dirt on the floor of his room?" He goes back to the room-examination section of the video. He zooms in on the floor beneath the window. Sure enough, there's no dirt there.

"Because no one ever came in?"

"Which means?"

I look at the screen again. "Ben went to the window and climbed out. Or he didn't leave through that window."

"Which means?" Grady's voice shifts to a higher pitch.

"He must know the person who took him."

"Exactly. So if we're working with that assumption, then what happened this morning makes way less sense." He starts a video recorded from the local news.

Erin and Jack Carter are standing outside their house, behind a podium. "Mayor Jack Carter and his wife will now speak to the press," a voice says.

Erin is wringing her hands and staring at the microphone. She leans in and speaks. "Our son, Ben Carter, disappeared Saturday night. We don't know where he is, but someone out there does. We would like to say to whoever has Ben that all we care about is him coming home safe. That's all. Whoever has Benny…" She stops and turns her face into the crumpled tissue in her hands.

"Our local law enforcement is doing an incredible job here," Jack says, sounding every bit the politician. "They have been on top of this since minute one. But now we need your help. If anyone has any information about Benjamin or the situation surrounding his disappearance, please, contact the local police force immediately." He throws an arm around Erin's shoulders. "We just want our son to come home safe."

Grady shuts the video down and laughs.

"You find the strangest things amusing," I say.

"Heartfelt, wasn't it?"

"I guess."

He clicks a file on the laptop, and an audio clip begins.

"We have Ben. For one million dollars, you can have him back. We will be in contact." The voice is muffled and high-pitched.

"What was that?" I say.

"That was a ransom call," Grady says. "It came an hour before the heartfelt plea."

"Today?"

"Yes, today."

"Has anything been released about it?"

"Not that I've seen," Grady says. "I imagine these kinds of calls often happen when a kid goes missing. Someone decides there's a chance to make some money and jumps at it. So it might not be legit. But then again, it might be. What is interesting about it is this." Grady plays the clip again, somehow slowing it down. It's almost as if he's able to lengthen the sound. "Hear that?"

"What?"

"In the background." I listen more carefully. There's a bit of a whine in the distance. A steady grinding noise.

"What is that?" I say.

"An electric sander. The kind used on cars." Grady rolls away from the desk and grabs a giant tool. He pulls a trigger and the same whining sound whips up. "Like this one."

"Do you have Ben in here somewhere?" I say.

"No. Sorry. I've never even seen the kid except on TV." He rolls over to me and takes my hands. "If I had him, I'd give him to you."

"How sweet. So what does the grinding have to do with anything?"

"Two things," Grady says, releasing my hands. "First, did you know that JJ Carter was once a well-known street racer?"

"Like in cars?"

"What other types of street racing are there?" he asks, as if I know some secret and am keeping it from him.

"I don't know," I say. "Skateboards? Bikes? Big Wheels?"

"Cars. JJ raced cars on city streets. Anyway, about a year ago another street racer died in a single-car accident out on Beacon Hill Road."

"And?"

"*And* oddly, that very same day, JJ's car was reported stolen." Grady pulls a police report up on his computer. I look at the scribbled mess of writing. "I found this in Detective Evans's files. When she got the missing-kid case, she pulled everything on the family from the records. Right down to parking tickets."

"Sounds like quite the coincidence. Do you think it was a coincidence?"

"I don't believe in coincidences," Grady says.

I try to figure out if he's being serious. "That doesn't make sense. It's like saying you don't believe in, I don't know, air."

"Actually, it isn't. It's like saying I believe everything that happens is part of a string of events that culminates in some final event we actually pay attention to."

"So what do you think happened?"

"In the newspaper reports of the accident, someone said they saw another car on the hill that night." Grady scrolls through the local paper's archive. "Right here. The only problem is that JJ was *apparently* safe at home, and *apparently* his car had been stolen that afternoon."

"I remember his car being stolen," I say. "He bitched about it for weeks afterward. Then said he wasn't going to get a new one until he found the right ride."

"Has he?"

"Not that I know of. Are you thinking that JJ had something to do with this other kid's death?"

"They were both street racers. And it's pretty convenient timing, isn't it?"

"But what does this have to do with the ransom call?"

"Maybe nothing, but my uncle told me that JJ's been wanting to open a high-end chop shop for a while. You know, pimping rides, putting big engines in old Pontiacs, that kind of thing. JJ's been looking at a location in that weird industrial mall in the west end. My uncle sends work to this guy Hank who has a body shop out there."

"What would that have to do with Ben?"

Grady's genuine smile comes out again, and he says, "*Fargo.*"

"Who?"

"The movie *Fargo.*"

"I don't know that one," I admit.

"It's about this guy who needs money but can't ask his rich father-in-law for it because he's too embarrassed and knows his father-in-law will never give it to him. So he hires a couple of guys to kidnap his wife and demand a ransom from her father."

"How does that work?" I say.

"He asks for twice what he needs. The plan is to split it fifty-fifty with the hired kidnappers, and his wife comes home safe and sound."

"Does she?"

"No," Grady says. "Which is why we have to go."

"Where?" I say. "Where are we going now?"

"If I'm right, we're going to bring Ben back."

TWENTY-ONE

The possible chop shop is empty—though calling it empty doesn't do it justice. It is utterly deserted but for a For Lease sign on the window. This area would have once been referred to as the outskirts, but businesses and apartment buildings have been closing in. Unfortunately, this little industrial mall doesn't seem any less weird for its proximity to civilization.

"Nothing here," Grady says, coming away from the window.

"Should we break in?" I say. I get a look from Grady.

"You can see the whole space from here. I don't think committing a crime is necessary."

I put my hands to the window and look inside at the big empty space. Grady is right—there's nowhere to hide.

"Dammit, and here I was getting all ramped up for a little criminal activity." There's a steady grinding sound coming from farther along the complex.

"I'm sorry. I thought we would find him this time," Grady says.

"It was a good idea."

"Let's go talk to Hank," Grady says, walking toward the noise.

The final unit of the complex is double the size of any of the other spaces. There are two cars up on lifts and another one parked beside the doors. A man in dirty blue coveralls is working on the trunk of an old Mustang.

Grady leans into his peripheral vision. The guy jumps and shuts the sander down. He flips his goggles up onto his forehead. "Help you?" he asks.

"Hey, you're Hank, right?" Grady says.

The guy sets the sander on the ground and leans back against the car. "Yeah?" His voice is smoker heavy.

"My uncle, Rodney, sends stuff your way sometimes," Grady says.

The guy flicks a pack of cigarettes out of a shirt pocket. He gets one out and lights it with a lighter from inside the pack. "You're Rodney's nephew? Yeah, he's talked about you some." The guy pauses for a moment. "Is your name Gravy?"

"Grady. With a d." Grady hiccups a little laugh.

"Your uncle's got a lisp on him, doesn't he? I always thought he was saying Gravy. Good to finally meet you and put that mystery to rest." He extends his hand, and Grady steps forward to shake it. "What can I help you with?"

"We were wondering if you'd seen JJ Carter around here. His stepbrother is missing," I say.

"I didn't know that."

Which is really surprising. With all the news about it because Ben is the mayor's son, I find it hard to believe that anyone wouldn't have heard by now.

"He was here earlier today, actually," Hank says.

"JJ?"

"Yeah, the little shit."

"Was he wanting to rent one of the spaces in this complex?"

"Rent? Nah, he came in as a *courtesy*." He gives little air quotes here, flicking away some ash as he does so. "Says he's gonna own the whole place soon enough. He'll be opening his own shop down the far end. Specialize in making ugly cars go faster than they should. Put stupid rims on Subarus. That shit. He was looking around my space like he already owned it."

"When was this?" I ask.

"Like I said, this morning," Hank says.

"Did he have a little kid with him?"

"Nope, he came in alone. There was someone else in the car with him. An older guy. He stayed put."

"Were you sanding this car this morning when he was here?" Grady says.

Hank looks at the Mustang. "I've been sanding this car for two straight days. The most delicate piece of work I have ever had the misfortune of undertaking."

"Okay, thanks," Grady says. "Sorry to bother you."

"No worries. Tell Rod I say hi and that I have that Subaru ready for him whenever he wants it."

"Will do," Grady says.

Hank flips down his goggles and revs the electric sander back to life, and we walk away.

Grady stops while we're passing the empty unit. "If we were inside there, the sander would sound muffled, just like the one on the ransom call."

"You think JJ has Ben?" I say.

"Maybe," Grady says. "Do you?"

"It's possible, but JJ is always so full of hot air that I imagine he's trying to use the situation to his advantage." I look in the window again.

"How could he think he's going to open a garage here?" Grady asks. "Where is that coming from?"

"Maybe Daddy doesn't want him around cars after what happened and won't lend him the money for his own shop. Like you were saying before about that *Furgo* movie."

"*Fargo*," Grady says. "Where does that leave us?"

I pull away from the window and look Grady in the eye. "Nowhere," I say.

TWENTY-TWO

Grady drops me at home and I spend the afternoon watching *Fargo*. My mother comes home, exhausted and hungry. I make her my special Hamburger Helper stew, and then we settle in to watch *Survivor*. It's something we've done since I was a kid and always makes me feel at home.

Neither of us says a word about Tom or Ben or even flicks to the news. I don't feel as though we're avoiding it either. It's just that there really is nothing we can do. Not at this moment anyway.

Halfway through the second episode, my cell vibrates. I pull it out of my pocket and answer without looking at the name. "Hello?"

"He has an uncle."

It's Grady. I climb out from under the blanket my mother and I have stretched over us and walk to my room.

"Who?"

"Ben. He has, like, not an *uncle* uncle, but a *step*-uncle."

"A step-uncle?" I say.

"Jack has a stepbrother," Grady says.

"I don't think that's true," I say. "I mean, I've never heard about this."

"That's because Jack's never told anyone. Or maybe he has. Let's say the news outlets don't know, because it would be incredible information if they did."

"Why?"

"Because he's an ex-con."

"What?" I say.

"His name is Joe. He's five years older than Jack. His father—get this: Jack and Joe's father led this crazy double life. He lived out west in Seattle for most of his life. He knocked this woman up before skipping town. He bounced around the States for a while before settling here and, very quickly, knocking Jack's mother up."

"At which time he stayed?"

"He married, settled down and, I guess, left that old life behind."

"How do you know all this?"

"I had to trace Jack's father, Don Carter. Luckily, he was drawing a GI disability check before he moved here. He was injured in the Second World War. So that wasn't too difficult to follow back. I did a little research into the high school and college and everything else. I found people he knew, looked them up and kept going. One guy he he was in the army with told me about the high-school sweetheart Jack's dad left behind. So I called her."

"You called some old woman? She must be in her eighties or nineties."

"Ninety-seven. Anyway, all I had to do was say *Don Carter*, and it all came out. The whole mess of a story. Her name is Martha Fisher. She admitted that Don was her son's father. Then she told me about her son Joe."

"Jack's stepbrother."

"Yeah. Jack's stepbrother. I asked where he was, and she said she didn't know. That he'd left years ago and hadn't spoken to the family since. There'd been a disagreement, apparently. She didn't get into it. But with that I was able to take the guy's name, Joe Fisher, and follow him around the United States."

"You did this all this afternoon?"

"No, not all of it. I'd been trying to put this together before. It seemed weird because he kind of came out of nowhere."

"And you didn't tell me because...?" I say.

"It might not have led anywhere. And anyway, Don's dead. But you said Detective Evans suggested Ben's disappearance would have something to do with a family member. Right?"

"Family first."

"So I investigated the family."

"*And?*" I was getting a little impatient.

"As far as I can tell, when Joe left Seattle he fell straight into a life of crime. He went to jail in Denver for car theft. He robbed a 7-Eleven in Las Vegas. A couple more cars. I mean, these are the crimes he was busted for. And drug dealing in New York. He did five years for that, but he's been out for two."

"And now where is he?"

"That's what I've been working on. Tracking this guy wasn't hard. There's information about everything he has done. But he suddenly disappeared. The next thing I know, I found a couple of personal checks being written to Joe on Jack Carter's personal account."

"How did you get into his personal account?"

"He left his Wi-Fi open, remember? He's even left himself logged in to his bank account a few times lately," Grady says.

I sit down on my bed and look out the window. It's getting dim out, that purple time of evening. "How much were these checks for?"

"One was for $3,000 and then a week later there was one for $800." I hear some crashing around on Grady's end. When he comes back, he's speaking even more quickly. "The checks were just the beginning. I had to go back to when Jack became mayor to really look into what was going on."

"You're losing me."

"When you become a public official, like a mayor or senator or whatever, you have to give up any business that you could use your power to influence."

"Such as?" I get off the bed and stand at the window. Some kids are playing road hockey in front of my house. I watch them pushing and shoving one another, sticks flashing in the evening light.

"Real estate, mostly. I mean, that's the big one."

"And did Jack Carter do that?"

"He had a lot of investments before he became the mayor. He was on the board of Racmar Homes, which does about three quarters of the construction in town. He also personally owned a lot of property. So when he became mayor, he had to leave the board and sell his shares in Racmar."

"So he gave all that up to be mayor?"

"He didn't have a choice. Every new building in town would be a conflict of interest for him. He didn't have to sell his personal property though. If it came to building on land he owned, he'd have to declare a conflict of interest and keep out of any negotiations with the building companies, but there was nothing wrong with him holding on to the properties. What's really strange is that one of these properties is outside the city limits."

"Why's that strange?"

"Because he didn't have to sell it," Grady says. He has that excited jingle in his voice again.

"You just said he didn't have to sell any of his private property."

"Right, okay," Grady says. "He wouldn't have to sell anything that was, like, a house or apartment building. Land that was set to be developed had to be sold. But only if it was inside the city limits. He can own anything he wants outside of Resurrection Falls."

"But you're saying he sold this other property?"

"Yes, he did."

"And you know who he sold it to?"

"I do," he says.

"Tell me it's Joe Fisher."

"You are correct, dear Lauren. It was Joe Fisher. I actually knew that a while ago, but it didn't set off any alarm bells. So when I was researching Jack's father and went all the way back to Seattle…"

"And then heard the name Martha Fisher…"

"It connected. Right," he says.

One of the kids scores a goal, and the rest argue about it. I turn away from the window and sit at my desk.

Grady is silent for a moment. I let him be silent. When he finally speaks, he comes out with, "The thing is, everything is about wanting. If you can promise someone they'll get what they want, they'll do anything for you."

"What does that have to do with this?"

"Jack wants something. I'm guessing it's power. Control. I don't believe people who are uninterested in power go into politics. What does Joe want though? That's the real question."

"He wants to be part of this deal, I guess," I say. "For the money."

"Maybe," Grady says, though he doesn't sound convinced.

"Where is this property we're talking about anyway?"

"That's the best part, Lauren," Grady says, sounding excited again.

"What? What is the best part?"

"Are you interested in going for a little drive?"

—— —— —— ——

Forty-five minutes later, we're parked in the middle of the lot outside the weird industrial mall. There are a couple of baker's vans and an old pickup that looks as though it hasn't moved in months. Otherwise, it's a ghost town.

"What are we doing here?" I ask.

"This is one of the proposed locations for super-high-speed Internet," Grady says. He shuts the car off and we stare at the building in silence.

"For what?"

"A geek's dream. Really fast download speeds. So fast you wouldn't be able to tell if something was on your computer or on the Internet."

"Okay, so what?"

"It will help bring major businesses here. Web designers and online innovation companies. There'll be tax breaks as well." Grady turns back to the complex. "This area could be one of the next places to get those kinds of speeds. Right now, only Kansas City has it."

I shake my head. "What would a chop shop and a bakery and a portrait framer and a used-furniture place want with super-high-speed Internet? Half of these stores are closed."

"That might be the point," Grady says. "Jack Carter has been lobbying heavily for this to happen here. It has to go through Google and the telecom companies and everything first. But the underground infrastructure is here already. There were tunnels drilled for sewage and water that were never used. It's the setup necessary to bring super-high-speed fiber wires in here."

"But why here?"

"There are plans in city council to build a campus for Internet start-ups and other uber-geeky companies. So whoever owns this building will be in line to make a mint. Think about it." His fingers are going on the steering wheel again. His hair is a bit floppy, as if he hasn't had time to deal with it. He's changed into a hoodie, jeans and blue Converse All Stars.

"I'm thinking," I say. "Okay, I've got nothing."

"What you have is condos coming in from that direction. There are plans for three towers in the next year. Trendy little shops and restaurants are opening along

Draper Road. If this space turned into a high-tech center, we'd be looking at one of the coolest, most advanced communications hubs in the country. The tech world in California has reached its peak. There's no space left for all the businesses, and a lot of companies have been looking for somewhere else to open data centers." He points at the building. "This could be it."

"Who owns it?" I ask. I'm pretty sure I already know the answer.

"A numbered company—181572, to be exact. It took a little digging to get to the bottom of it. It felt like a front from the beginning. There's a real-estate company involved, a couple of landowners, but they're all working under the umbrella of this company called Otomo."

"Like, Otomo Lake?" I say.

"Exactly."

"And who is Otomo?"

Grady looks at me.

I look back.

"You know the answer."

"Joe Fisher," I say.

"Exactly. What do you think the possibility is that Joe is being shafted by his brother and has become desperate or angry about it? Maybe something in the deal has fallen apart, and Joe feels left out. Or the mayor is suddenly afraid that he's made a mistake in trusting his half brother. So Joe has decided to take matters into his own hands. What leverage would he have? He couldn't suddenly turn his brother in. That would leave him with nothing."

"You think Joe may have kidnapped Ben?" I say.

"If he did, then Jack would know exactly where he was."

"What? Where?"

"You said it yourself. Otomo Lake. There's one tiny cottage there."

"That doesn't explain how Joe would have gotten Ben out of the house," I say. "I mean, would they even have met?"

"Yeah, that was bothering me as well. But if Joe had found out about the difficulties between Jack and JJ, he could have easily placed himself between the two of them. All he would have to do is tell JJ he could help him get what he wanted."

"The shop," I say. "Joe could help JJ get the shop he wants."

"And all JJ had to do," Grady says, "is help Joe borrow Ben for a couple of days. Help get him out of the house."

"JJ would see no problems with that, I bet," I say. "And Ben's such an easygoing kid, he would have gone with JJ."

Grady starts the car and pulls out of the parking lot. "It all adds up," he says. "Joe is Jack's caretaker on this property. He also owns the Otomo Lake area. It's a perfect fit."

"How so?"

"Think about it," Grady says for the eight hundredth time. "You buy this area and get the high-tech firms in here.

The little cubicle zombies put in their hours, then go back to their little dinkpads down the street..."

"Dinkpads?" I say.

"Double income, no kids, probably a dog. Dinkpads." He laughs. "Dinks are a marketer's dream. They like all-inclusive holidays, long walks on the beach, retro gear of any description, soy lattes and are as flush with cash as all other demographics put together. But the one thing they desire more than anything else is a place to unwind. A little spot of their own with some trees, a beach and water to stare at."

"A place not too far away," I say, starting to understand. We're hurtling down the highway. Headlights are coming on as the purple sky darkens to black.

"An hour with traffic," Grady says. "A quick drive outside of town but with the feeling that you're hundreds of miles from civilization."

"Otomo Lake," I say.

"Otomo Lake."

TWENTY-THREE

Once you leave the highway, only a single road cuts through the Otomo Lake area. It's little more than a series of dirt paths. This particular dirt path seems remarkably well traveled.

It's too dark to tell exactly what is around us, but as the car bounces on the rough road, the headlights illuminate flashes of massive trees and bushes. Branches reach out above the road, though many have been snapped off and tossed to the side or crushed into the dirt.

"Look at those tracks," I say, leaning forward as Grady slows the car down. "They're huge." We come around a corner and discover what has been so angrily destroying nature.

There are three semitrucks loaded with trees parked on the right side of a split. Grady cuts to the left and stops once we're safely behind some brush. He shuts the car off, and we sit in the resulting silence.

"What is going on back there?" I say.

"It looks like clear-cutting to me," Grady says.

We get out of the car. The clicking of branches clipping one another in the wind and the scurrying of animals through the underbrush take over from the hum of the wheels on the road. We stay close to the larger trees on the side of the road, though it seems unlikely that anyone would be working at this time.

It's a clear enough night that the moon illuminates the lakefront area.

"It looks like they're making room for cottages or a resort or something," Grady says.

There is no sign of life around the trucks and machinery. "Wouldn't you need permits for this?" I say.

Grady spots something across the road. He runs over to a tree with a giant orange X on it. "Not if the trees are diseased," he says.

There are X's everywhere. Tall, healthy-looking trees marked for destruction.

"I'm not a botanist or anything, but they look fine to me," I say. "You said there was a cottage or something here?"

"Yes," Grady says. He looks at his cell. "It's this way."

We leave the car and walk the rest of the way. The road here is less worn. The branches above our heads are so full that the sky is no longer visible.

Grady stops a couple of times to look at the ground. "It's hard to tell, but these tracks look pretty new."

After a final corner, we discover the cottage. It's a one-story place with a broken-down barn across from it.

Someone could come along at any moment, and we'd be trapped. The thought makes my stomach drop.

There is an old Volkswagen Jetta and a silver BMW parked beside the cottage. Calling it a cottage seems a bit much. It's a shack with two windows and a door on the back wall, all three glowing from lights inside.

"Someone's here," I say. We slip into the forest and crouch beside a tree. I try to breathe slowly. It is ridiculously difficult. I close my eyes, tip my head to the sky and then refocus on the world around me. *This is important*, I think. *Pull yourself together.*

"It has to be Joe," Grady says. There's a small window in the barn. I move a little closer to the window and look in.

Freeze.

Pull back.

"What kind of car is that in there?" I say.

Grady takes my place at the window. "It looks like a white Ford Taurus."

"Like the car that was apparently stolen from JJ?"

"Exactly like that," Grady says. Neither of us moves.

"We should go see if there's a door at the back," I say.

"We should," Grady says without moving.

"Then we need to look inside the cottage."

"I guess we do," Grady says. His voice is quivering.

I take his hand. "So come on." I hear him inhale. I let go of his hand and move along the side of the barn. Luckily, there is a door. There's only an empty hole where the doorknob should be. I slip my fingers through and pull the door open enough to slip in beside JJ's stolen car.

"The bastard," I say. I feel the hairs stand up on my arms. I didn't know the kid who died on Beacon Hill Road that night, but looking at this car is the same as finding a gun used in a murder. Or a bloody knife. This was a weapon, no matter how you look at it.

And JJ was the killer.

Grady has his phone out and is taking pictures. "That's the car, isn't it?"

"Yes," I say. Every time he takes a photo, the flash goes off.

"You're sure?"

"How many of these could there be in town?" I say.

"Tons," Grady says. "Trust me there." He looks out the window while pulling his sleeve over his hand.

"What are you doing?" I say.

He opens the driver's side door. "Keep an eye out for anyone coming this way. I want to get a closer look." He pops the hood and walks to the front of the car. "This is a major engine," he says. "Seriously tricked out." He sets the hood down, then pushes it as quietly as possible back into place. "I think we'll have to sit on this. No newspaper is going to run a story about JJ Carter's stolen car." Grady pockets his phone. "It would seem incredibly insensitive at a time like this. Plus, there is no proof he had anything to do with that other kid's death."

"Maybe if it's given to them the right way," I say. "If the police aren't telling the public everything…"

"If I learned anything from that whole situation with my dad, it's that the police and media work together," Grady says. "No reporter is going to kill his connection with the mayor's office or the police to run something like this. There's too much at stake."

We move around the car to the front of the barn and look out a filthy window.

"What if we sent it to someone out of town? Someone in Albany or over in Vermont?"

"Media is all about connections. We'd have to find someone with a really serious grudge against the Carters."

"That's possible," I say hopefully. "There must be people out there that he's pissed off."

"With Benny missing, I really doubt many newspapers would take the risk to attack a man."

"It can hold," I say. "We have this now—we can use it."

"Listen to you," Grady says. "What are you thinking?"

"There has to be someone inside." I shift a little and knock a wrench off the workbench. It clangs on the floor, and we freeze. Grady grabs my hand. For what seems like forever, neither of us breathes.

"Come on, let's…" I begin.

Then someone comes banging out of the cottage, yelling, "It never works up here. I have to go down by the lake."

We duck. We crouch there for a moment before slowly straightening to look out the window.

JJ Carter stands in the halo of light from the doorway, his cell phone above his head, looking at the glowing screen. "If we do it here, we'll lose the connection."

"Fine." A man appears in the doorway. He lights a cigarette as he comes down the steps. "Let's go down to the water."

JJ brings the phone closer to him. "Like that, I lose the signal," he says. He raises the phone again. "There, I have it. It's so messed up."

"You can't float six feet off the ground to call him," the other man says. He's shaking his head at JJ. "Just go to the lake."

"You're coming with me," JJ says. "I'm not explaining all this to him myself."

"You can't talk to your father on your own?"

"Not about this. I don't understand half of this stuff."

"Go," the guy says, giving JJ a shove.

"That's Joe Fisher," Grady says. "I've seen his mug shot."

I grab Grady's hand and say, "We have to go inside."

"Why?"

"Because Ben could be in there."

"What if they come right back?"

"We can't think about it," I say. "We have to go now. Come on." I run out the rear door of the garage, then crouch and move as quickly and quietly as possible to the back of the cottage. I look around the corner and see, a few hundred feet down toward the beach, JJ and Joe sitting on a log. For some reason, I'm not all that nervous suddenly. There's a pounding in my ears, and I'm clenching my teeth, but I feel as though I can do anything.

"You stay here and watch," I say to Grady.

"What? You're going in alone?"

"Someone has to be the lookout."

"You be the lookout. If they come back, you warn me and run to the car."

I have to think fast. "No. Because Ben doesn't know you. If he's in there, why would he go with you?" Grady opens his mouth to protest, but I interrupt. "We don't have time to argue. If they start coming, let me know." I run inside before he can say another word.

I'm standing in the kitchen. There's a passageway to a living room and then two bedrooms on either side of what has to be a bathroom. Both bedroom doors are open.

I stay low and crawl through the passage to the living room. The place is a mess of empty bottles and cigarette butts. Magazines and newspapers are scattered on the floor. A PlayStation 3 is plugged into a small TV.

The bedroom on the right is all bedsheets, ashtrays and empty beer and whiskey bottles. I look in the closet and find it entirely empty.

Before I leave, I take a quick glance out the window. JJ and Joe are still down by the water, their forms silhouetted against the moon.

The other bedroom is cleaner, though not by much. A bed has been tipped upright against the wall to make room for a large desk and chair.

I open a drawer and discover batteries, keys and empty cigarette packs. The other drawer is empty. I reach around inside and find nothing.

I sense someone at the window and quickly duck.

"What are you doing?" Grady whisper-yells. "Is he in there?"

"No," I say.

"Then get out. Come on."

"Just a minute."

"What are you doing?"

"Just keep watching for them."

I open the first drawer again.

Nothing has changed. I want to turn the light on. Instead, I bring out my phone and use the flashlight app. I suddenly don't care if Joe or JJ eventually discovers I was in here. None of it really matters. I need to find something. Something that can tell us what to do next.

I go to the empty drawer again and move my hand around the space.

"Lauren, they're coming," Grady whisper-yells.

It has to be here, I say to myself. *It has to.* As I'm pulling my hand out, I twist it so my fingers are on the underside of the drawer. At first I don't feel anything, but then, as I slide my hand out, my nail catches on something. I shift a little and find a small, hard rectangle held on by tape. I tear at the tape and pull out a little red USB drive.

"What are you doing here?"

I turn to find JJ standing in the doorway.

He takes a step toward me. "You bitch, what are you holding?" He points at my hand. He takes another step toward me. He looks angrier than I've ever seen him. There is pure hatred in his eyes. "I asked you a question."

"You tried to blame everything on Tom," I say, "when all along you knew he had nothing to do with your brother's disappearance."

"He has Ben," JJ says. "I'm certain."

"I know what you're doing out here," I say. I hold up the USB drive. "This is all the proof I need."

"But you're not going anywhere with it," JJ says. He moves toward me, his hand out. I wait until the right moment, then bring my foot up hard into his groin. He crumples to the floor, unsuccessfully attempting to reintroduce air to his lungs. I feel like kicking him in the head. Like stomping on his face for all that he's done and all he'll likely do. For everything he gets away with because of who he is. But I know it would do no good and wouldn't make me feel any better.

Anyway, I got what I wanted.

I jump over JJ and dart through the house and out the door. Grady is still beneath the window.

"Let's go!" I say.

We're halfway to Grady's car when I hear Joe yell, "What the hell happened to you?"

TWENTY-FOUR

"I never turned it around," Grady yells as he gets in the driver's seat.

"There isn't anywhere *to* turn around," I say, slamming the passenger door closed. Through the darkness, headlights flare up. They dance around the woods, illuminating the trees and the road and the interior of Grady's car.

Grady jams the car into reverse, throws an arm over the seat and starts backing down the trail. The BMW's headlights are blinding. Branches bang against the roof. The car heaves along the track, engine squealing. Within seconds the BMW is on us, so close I can make out JJ's angry face behind the steering wheel.

"He's going to ram us," I say.

Joe is beside JJ. He has a cigarette trapped between his lips and looks for all the world as if he's out for a Sunday drive.

"I can't go any faster," Grady says. When we break into the open area at the split, Grady cuts hard to the right and spins around in a graceful arc.

JJ flies past, sliding sideways as he brakes hard and comes to a stop in a cloud of dust.

"He's blocking our way out," I say. Grady's eyes are darting all over the place. He drops the car into *drive* and guns it, steering straight toward the BMW. "Grady!" I yell. Both cars skid from side to side as they approach one another. At the last second, Grady cuts to the right and slides around the back of the BMW, then swerves up a little rise and back onto the track.

"Holy crap," I say.

Grady steers down the track, bringing the car back under control.

It doesn't take long for JJ to catch up in the bigger, more powerful BMW. We bang out onto the side road in a wash of dirt and dust, headlights flashing all over the place. Two quick turns later and we're on the highway. Grady accelerates around a U-Haul, cutting off a minivan in the process.

"I won't be able to outrun a BMW in this piece of junk," he says.

"So what are we going to do?" I say.

Grady keeps checking his side mirror. "We're okay for a few minutes. He's stuck behind that U-Haul." The minivan edges up to pass us, and Grady shifts back into the passing lane to cut him off. The minivan's horn roars through the open windows. The only way JJ could get to us right now would be to drive on the shoulder.

"We can't do this all the way back to town," I say. "Eventually, he'll be right beside us."

"I know, I know," Grady says. "Let me think for a minute." He keeps checking the mirrors, speeding up and slowing down.

I look at the side mirror and see the BMW switching lanes. Grady lets off the gas for a moment, and the U-Haul driver sounds a long horn.

"The old highway comes off the next overpass. You have to drive through Morrisberg to get to it. After that, it's a straight shot north back into Resurrection Falls."

"But there isn't an off-ramp on this side of the road," I say, as the overpass comes into view.

"No," Grady says. "There isn't." The minivan driver sounds the horn again as Grady's hand goes to the parking brake between our seats.

"What are you doing?"

"Hold on," he says. He begins to accelerate, pulling away from the U-Haul and the minivan.

"Grady," I say. "What are you doing?"

"Sit loose. Don't get all tense."

"Why?" I say. "What are you going to do?"

His hand tightens on the parking brake. His eyes are wide, and he seems to be breathing more quickly than necessary.

"Grady?" I say again.

As we drive beneath the shadow of the overpass, Grady yanks the parking brake and turns hard to the left, sliding off the road. We're heading directly toward a cement stanchion when he releases the brake, cuts hard to the left and swerves around it. We come out onto the other side of the highway in a long sideways slide, weaving in between two cars. Grady works the steering wheel back and forth in an attempt to straighten out. The problem is, we're driving in the wrong direction on the only highway in the area. It's late, but not late enough for the road to be empty. He steers back to the shoulder, the rear tires slipping on the loose gravel.

"Grady!" I yell.

The BMW is keeping pace with us on the other side of the highway. We reach the off-ramp as a wall of cars crest the rise in the road ahead of us.

Grady's hand goes to the parking brake again, and the next thing I know we're doing a one-eighty slide across the road to a chorus of horns, narrowly making it onto the off-ramp. Grady releases the parking brake and straightens the car out while slowing down.

"Where did you learn to drive like that?" I say.

"You don't want to know." His hair has flopped to one side, and a trickle of sweat is making its way down his cheek.

"I do," I say. "Or I wouldn't have asked." We cross the overpass, and I can see the lights of the BMW as JJ brakes and swerves into the right lane.

"*GTA*," Grady says.

"The video game?"

"And the *Need for Speed* games too. I drive those on ultra-realistic mode."

"You've never done anything like that before?"

Grady exhales, shaking his head. "No way. That was crazy!"

"But you decided it was a good time to start?"

"I guess so," he says. And then he starts laughing. He reaches over and pats my leg. "In theory it seemed like it would work. And somehow it did!"

"You're a maniac," I say.

— — — —

Morrisberg is a small town, which, if the current development continues, will soon be part of Resurrection Falls. Its little stores and cafés are cute and quaint and will likely be torn down and turned into strip malls. A traffic light switches to red ahead of us. Grady turns in to a parking lot, weaves through some cars and pops out onto a side street.

I'm shaking from what has happened. From sneaking into the cottage to confronting JJ to the crazy driving. My nerves feel shaved. I suddenly notice I've been holding the handle above the door. I bring my hand down, and my knuckles are pure white.

My cell buzzes. I pull it out of my pocket, wondering who would be contacting me.

It's a text: **Tom has been spotted. DE**

"What?" I say, almost dropping the phone in surprise. She has to be lying.

"What?" Grady says.

"Detective Evans just texted me that Tom has been spotted."

"Find out where," Grady says.

I manage to get some composure back and say, "Should I be writing her? Shouldn't I turn my phone off so they can't track me?"

Grady looks in the rearview mirror. "I don't think having the police interested in us at the moment would be a horrible idea."

Where? I text.

My phone buzzes again.

Come to the station.

"She's not going to tell me," I say. I start flipping through web pages to see if there is anything online. We're bumping along a pothole-filled mess of a road, which makes selecting links and reading next to impossible.

"How the hell did he catch up?" Grady says, looking in the rearview mirror again. I turn and see the silver BMW coming up behind us. "He must be driving like a maniac."

"Said the pot to the kettle," I say. "Where can we lose him?"

"Maybe the industrial park," Grady says. "But if he catches us in there, we're totally screwed."

"No, we need somewhere public." I keep scanning the news sites for information about Tom, and finally I find something on Twitter. "They think Tom's downtown."

"Where?"

"It doesn't say Tom is there. But someone's tweeting that there's a major police presence in the 800 block of Fallgate near Toluse." I stare at the screen for a moment, thinking. We're on the outskirts of Resurrection Falls, driving past the endless line of big-box stores. The downtown core is maybe ten minutes away if we go straight and hit all green lights. Grady blows a red light, and JJ follows right along behind us.

Grady is right: there's no way we can lose him.

"We're screwed," Grady says. He sighs. "But what does it matter?"

"What do you mean?"

"They're closing in on Tom, right?"

"You don't think all of this matters?"

"What can we do about it, Lauren?"

"He hid the fact that his son had something to do with a kid's death? That doesn't bother you?"

"We don't know that for certain," Grady says, suddenly turning right.

"Where are you going?"

"I'm taking you to the police station. This has all been about Tom from the beginning, right? To make certain he was okay. To find out where he went and why. Well, if the police have found him, then you need to go there. To help him."

"No," I say. I hold the USB drive out toward Grady. "There's more to it than that." I pause for a moment, then say, "It's all on here."

"What is that?" he says. "Where did you get it?"

"Everything is on here." I wave it at him. "The payments, the payoffs, all the places the money went. I bet there's a payoff to the cop who put the wrong time down on JJ's incident report. If we don't get this out, it doesn't matter what happens to Tom or Ben—all of this will be buried forever."

Grady glances at the USB drive as we go under a streetlight. "Wait a second." He grabs the drive from me before I know what's happening. "This is a paired USB drive. You can't see what's on here unless you have both drives."

"I know," I say.

"How do you know that?" He hands me back the drive.

"I just do."

"What's going on, Lauren?"

"Go to the mayor's house," I say.

There's a long pause, which breaks my heart a little. Grady is trying to figure out what I know and how I know it. Wondering what secrets I've been keeping from him.

"What aren't you telling me, Lauren?" he asks.

I close my fist around the drive. "You have to trust me, Grady," I say. "I can make this right. But you need to get me there as fast as you can."

TWENTY-FIVE

We're driving through my suburban world.

"You think the other flash drive is in the mayor's house?" Grady asks.

I say, "If the brothers are working together but didn't trust one another, they'd split the information exactly like this."

"But then every time someone wanted to work on the file, they'd have to be together."

"Which is where JJ stepped in," I say.

We're two blocks from the Carters' house. Grady stops at an intersection and looks both ways. The house on the corner has a giant hedge, which is impossible to see around. Grady looks at me as we pull into the intersection. He opens his mouth to say something, but the words never come out.

"Grady, look out!" I scream.

It happens so fast that my words are buried beneath the crunch of steel and the shattering of glass. We have rammed into a telephone pole, and the resulting jolt sends my entire body into the air, only to be yanked back down by the seat belt. I watch as my face comes within inches of the dash. The BMW, which must have been moving at an incredible pace, spins away from the pole and smashes into the back of a parked pickup.

The seat belt has held me tightly, but my neck feels as though it's been snapped. There's a ringing in my ears, and when the car was thrown sideways, I smashed my hand into something.

"Are you okay?" I say.

"I don't know." Grady holds his hands up before him. "What just happened?"

"He rammed us," I say.

I open my hand to find it empty. There are bits of broken glass all over my lap, but the windshield is a spiderweb of lines. It's the side window that is broken.

I undo my seat belt and look between my feet at the floor. "Where's the drive?" I say.

Grady looks at me like he's been hit in the head with a shovel. Which, I suppose, is not that far from what has actually happened.

"What?"

"The USB drive. Look for it, please."

Grady touches his head, then turns to his window. "There's JJ," he says.

I look up to see JJ falling out of his car. He lies there for a second before attempting to stand—without success. I go back to looking for the drive.

I move my hand around on the floor until I feel something slice into my thumb. "Shit," I say.

Grady is still staring out the window.

"I have to go," I say.

"What?" Grady mutters.

"Did you bang your head?"

He touches his head again. "No. I just…" His sentence stalls, and he goes back to staring at JJ on the ground outside his car.

"Tell me when he gets up," I say. I hammer on the door until it pops open. Already I can hear sirens cutting across the sky. People are coming out of their houses, calling out to one another.

"You're going to be okay," I say. "You're going to be fine. Everything is going to be fine."

My heart is going triple the speed it should. I slide out of the car and drop to my knees beside it. The drive has to be under the seat. It can't be outside the car—there's just no way.

Because without it, I'm lost.

Grady looks down at me, stunned.

"I can't go without that drive." I glance back up at Grady. "Grady, you have to help me."

"This?" he says, holding up the USB drive.

"Yes, that," I say. I reach out and take it from him. "Thank you."

"Sure." He points out the window. "JJ is coming over here."

"Don't worry about JJ," I say, clasping the flash drive. "This will all be over soon."

"Are you all right?" someone yells. I look up and see an older man with his hands on JJ's shoulders. "Son, are you okay?" There are people pouring onto the street now.

JJ stumbles as he pushes away from the man. There's a tear in his pant leg, and blood is staining his expensive shoes. I back away from the car. JJ looks at me, his eyes not quite focusing. The older man grabs him again and tells him he should sit down. JJ's uncle is still in the car. There is blood on his face, and he's not moving. The air bag has inflated on the driver's side, but not the passenger's. For some reason, the right turn signal is flashing.

I give JJ a quick smile as I hold the USB drive up.

I see the recognition on his face. What that little piece of plastic means.

"You'll never find it!" he yells.

But he's wrong. I already know exactly where the other USB drive is.

And I'm going to get it.

I turn and cut through the advancing crowd. Running as quickly and strongly as I ever have before.

—— —— —— ——

The patio door is open, and the alarm is off inside the Carters' house. I slip in as quietly as possible, even though I already know no one is home.

I go straight to Jack's den, a place I have only been once before, on the day Erin showed me the USB drive. There's a catch beneath the middle of his desk that unlocks a small compartment. I slide my hand along until I feel the hard plastic there and pull out the matching USB drive.

As I push the compartment back into place, I move the curtains aside to look out the window. An ambulance flashes past, followed by a cruiser. Lights go on in the driveway as another police car starts up. I hadn't thought anyone would be left outside the Carters' house. Luckily, I decided to go in the patio door.

The scream of sirens invades the house. A pulsing of noise, wave upon wave descending on the neighborhood. I wait at the doorway, listening. I thought I heard a sound. Footsteps, or the banging of the patio door closing. But there's no way that JJ, in his condition, would have been able to make it here. A firefighter or paramedic would have stopped him and forced him to sit down.

I pass Benny's room and look inside. It's clean, cleaner than any kid's room should be. But that is the way he likes it. I notice his stuffed elephant lying on the floor, slightly beneath the bed skirt. I go in and grab it, then run to the patio door. I stop for a moment, knowing I'll never be in this house again. Knowing that with all I have just done, everything has changed. But that it's changed for the better.

I turn toward my house but quickly realize the police will almost certainly be there. They'll be expecting Tom to run home. Plus, if JJ has been in contact with his father, the police will be looking for me by now as well. My name and picture popping up on all the little in-car computers.

I look up and down the street. There has to be somewhere I can go to download the information from the USB drives and still get away. Headlights break the darkness of the street, so I lean into the shadow surrounding a large maple tree on the Carters' lawn. The car slows, though it isn't a cruiser. It speeds up as it passes the house and a moment later is gone. I look at the sidewalk and wonder how many times I've walked these streets. How many times my feet have touched the earth.

Then I know exactly where I can go.

— — — —

Marlene looks at me there on her front porch.

"You look frazzled," she says. And I love her for it. I step inside, and she shuts the door. "Are you okay?"

"I'm sorry," I say.

"For what?"

"For the past two years. For suddenly no longer being your friend."

"You were with different people," she says. "Same here." She shrugs, as if my abandoning her was nothing more than a missed step along the road. Something neither of us could have seen coming but that doesn't change anything that came before.

"Well, I'm still sorry."

"And you still don't have to be." She smiles. She's as big as ever, but her whole family is big. I see her mom out jogging now and then, but she never seems to slim at all. Her brother is in the fifth grade and is already the size of a small tank.

Families just work that way.

"Can I use your computer?" I say.

"Sure." Again, without question. There's the sound of sirens as more emergency vehicles rip past the house.

"I wonder what that's all about," she says.

We go up to her room. It smells of lilacs and cinnamon, like the kind of place a good person spends time.

Marlene logs in to her computer, then sits on her bed where she can't see what is on the screen. "Should I ask what is going on?"

I put the USB drives into the computer and wait. "It's my brother," I say.

"Yeah, I heard about all that."

The directory window opens. At first there is nothing. Then tiny lights on each of the drives come on, and files fill the screen.

It's ridiculous. They didn't even bother to hide the names. The files are called things like *Payment from Centrum Construction* and *Balance for Andre Tree Removal*. There's one called *Proof of Bribes*.

I open up the Centrum file, which turns out to be a balance sheet of payments and expectations. It looks as if this particular company has already paid Jack Carter over two hundred thousand dollars for his vote and support in city council meetings.

And all the files are like this. As I read through them, a clearer picture appears: Jack's been playing construction companies against one another. Getting more and more cash as the stakes were raised.

And Grady was right. Jack has his sights set on that industrial complex as the next big Web-based business hub, and his land around Otomo Lake as the vacation spot of choice.

He's set to make millions after he leaves public office. Even if all of this came out once he was no longer mayor, it wouldn't matter. His brother would have been the official owner of the property. If anyone decided they'd been on the losing end of a deal, he would have proof that they bribed him—or, if these files could be seen a different way, attempted to bribe him.

He has rough building plans, payouts from different businesses interested in a spot in the reworked industrial complex—he's even accepted payments from professional cleaning services for the exclusive rights to the buildings. I expect it was his brother who was the face of all these deals. If anyone knew it was the mayor behind this, they'd be very hard pressed to prove it.

Unless, of course, they had these files.

"Do you have something there that's going to help your brother?" Marlene asks.

"Not really," I say. "But it's going to be a start." I log in to my web mail and bring up the addresses I have saved there. Ben Richer at the *Post*, Dawn Coarse at the *Sun*, Frank Hardy at the *Resurrection Falls Times*. I add reporters from the *New York Times* and the larger papers in Albany.

I add Detective Evans's address and start attaching files.

The subject line is simple: *Major Corruption in the Resurrection Falls Mayor's Office.*

Luckily, Jack created many of the documents on his work computer, so the files are date-stamped as well as having *Property of Jack Carter, Mayor*, tagged in the properties.

He must have been so sure he would get away with it all. That he was entirely untouchable.

I manage to get a quarter of the files attached before I reach the size limit. I send the document to Drafts and start on the next bunch of files.

"Can I ask you for a favor?" I say to Marlene.

"Sure," she says.

"Actually, two favors. First, I have to leave in a second. Can you send these emails once I'm out of here?"

"That sounds easy enough."

"Also, can I borrow your car?"

"No problem," Marlene says.

It just about makes me cry.

I had totally written this girl off. But there's still no hesitation on her part. She'll lend me her car. She'll help me out. And she won't even ask any questions.

"I'm trying to be a better person," I say.

"You've never been a bad person," Marlene says.

"Yeah, I have. But I'm trying to be better."

TWENTY-SIX

I am halfway downtown in Marlene's mint-green Volvo when Detective Evans texts me.

What are these e-mails?

I pull over to text back. **Another truth.**

I wait. The engine rumbles beneath me. Cars flash past.

These are personal files, she texts.

They are proof of what Jack Carter has been doing, I reply. **He's selling this town out for his own gain. If anyone has Ben, it's the mayor's brother, Joe.**

I wait again, my heart hammering. Now that it is all coming together, I'm anxious and afraid it will fall apart.

Her response pops up on my screen. **What are these pictures of a car I received earlier?**

A year ago JJ Carter's car was reported stolen, I type. **It wasn't stolen. It was likely involved in the death of Michael Brent on Beacon Hill Road and then hidden to conceal the crime. The mayor was aware of this as well.**

There's no reply, so I drive on toward downtown.

The glow of a dozen cruisers lights up the end of Fallgate Road. I take a right toward the river. There are people everywhere, and the driving is slow. I turn my face away from the other cars and the people on the sidewalks and hope I'm not too late.

Percy Street dead-ends near the rapids that give Resurrection Falls its name. I pull into the parking lot near the falls and shut off the engine.

Are you going to bring the mayor in for questioning? I text. **Did you know that Joe Fisher even existed? Will you be interviewing JJ Carter?** I wait for two minutes as the engine clicks and cools. I think back to something Grady said. Something so simple, so absolutely basic.

Everything is about wanting.

Everything.

And if you can promise someone they will receive the one thing they want, you can get anything from them.

I can bring you Tom, I text. **But only if Mayor Carter is in custody and explaining what those files are all about.**

I get an immediate response. **I can't promise that.**

Mayor Carter has to be at the police station before I bring Tom out. Otherwise, you will never find him. Ever.

Does he have Benjamin? she texts.

I laugh. Ben doesn't matter, and I know it. She wants Tom to be guilty. She wants him to be the monster she thinks he is. And she wants to be the hero who stops him.

She wants that more than anything.

The mayor in police custody first, I type. I wait for a response, and when it comes, I'm not the slightest bit surprised.

What is in this for you?

I look at the screen and type **Everything.** There's another long pause. I watch as police cars troll the streets. A group of officers enters the shops at the end of the block. This whole area has been abandoned for months. Every window little more than a dusty frame for For Rent signs. One shop after another closed as the big-box stores moved in on the edge of town and forced them out.

On his way to station, comes a text at last.

Promise?

Promise. Now where is your brother?

I'll bring him to you.

— — — —

I get out of the car and wait as the officers across the street break down the door of what was once a knife shop. That was all it sold—knives. There was one along here that only sold hot sauce, and another that had a dozen or so shirts on a rack and maybe another dozen pairs of shoes.

The night has cooled, and I wish I was wearing some-thing more. I turn back to Marlene's car and find a sweat-shirt on the backseat. It's big on me, but at least it's black and warm. I grab Ben's elephant from the passenger seat and stuff it inside the sweatshirt.

The streetlights are bright, leaving me fully exposed as I run across the street, trying to stay in the shadows. If I get spotted out here, at the very least I'll be turned away. At worst, someone will recognize me, and ten minutes from now I'll be sitting in a little room in the police station, trying to explain myself and all I've done.

The alley behind the buildings on Percy Street is filled with garbage bins. The walls are a riot of graffiti. The blurp of sirens breaks the silence, along with a muddle of words and sounds from walkie-talkies.

I stop when I find the door. There's still an old hand-made sign there. Nothing special at all. Just *Radicals Records* written on cardboard and taped in a spot above the door where rain can't get at it. I consider knocking, then open the door and step inside.

"Hello," I whisper. I can't see anyone at first. The darkness is more complete inside than out. I say it again. "Hello, Tom? Ben?" I turn on the flashlight app on my phone. Its circle of light brings out all the edges and corners of the room.

"What took you so long?" Tom says as he steps out from behind a cabinet. His hair seems to have grown in the few days since I last saw him. He's also sporting a bit of stubble, which makes me laugh. He seems so grown-up.

That is, until I notice his fingers are coated in orange Cheezies dust.

"Things did not go entirely as planned," I say.

Benny steps out from behind him. He has Cheezies dust on his fingers too, as well as all over his face.

"We have to go," I say. Ben rushes across the room and takes my hand. "Benny. How are you?" I pick him up and feel his little body shivering. Something drops inside me. A rock that has been sitting in the middle of my throat for days.

"I'm well," he says. It makes me laugh how polite and proper he is. He throws his arms around my neck. He smells like old milk and dirty socks.

"We have to get going," I tell him. "That's okay, right?"

"Yes," he says.

"Is there a safe way out?" Tom asks.

They've been staying in what was once the back room of the record shop. The owner left behind a fridge, a microwave and a single bed when he cleared out. There's a SpongeBob SquarePants sleeping bag on the floor, surrounded by coloring books, a Nintendo DS and a paperback edition of *His Dark Materials*.

I pull Benny's stuffed elephant out from beneath Marlene's sweatshirt and hand it to him.

"You forgot this," I say.

He lets go of me for a moment and hugs it. "Ricky!" he says. He wraps his arms around my neck again, squishing the elephant between us. "Thank you."

"The alley was clear when I came in," I say, looking up at my brother. "But the police are moving from building to building. It won't be long."

"Someone spotted me," Tom says. "Ben wanted chocolate milk, and I thought I could get out and back without a problem. It's only three doors down."

I squeeze Ben.

"I'm sorry, Lauren," Tom says.

I feel angry. Or not even angry—just annoyed that he didn't stick to the plan. But this is Tom to the core. He thinks about others first. And he's always trying to save people.

"Where's my mom?" Ben says. "Tom said you'd bring her."

"She's waiting for you, Benny. You'll see her in a minute." I open the door and peer up and down the alley. I can hear banging and sirens in the distance. The rumble of walkie-talkies. It's possible that we cut it too close.

"Okay, come on," I say, gathering Ben up in my arms and stepping out.

We move from one garbage bin to another, staying low and trying to be as quiet as possible. It's difficult carrying Ben, but he doesn't seem to want to let go.

And I don't want to put him down.

We make it to the end of the alley just as a heavy flashlight beam breaks the darkness. I pull my cell phone out and put it on vibrate. The last thing I need is for it to suddenly go off and attract attention. We lean against the wall and wait as the bark of voices from the walkie-talkies battles it out. The sound of officers hammering on doors echoes in the alley. I can feel my body reacting to every thump. All it would take is one officer looking around a corner. Maybe a team is moving up the alley as we stand here. I wish there were someone who could tell me what to do now. Tom is stumbling along behind me, numbed from days of sitting quietly with a five-year-old. I'm so exhausted I can't see straight.

"Okay," I say. Ben leans back to look around. His eyes are huge. I wonder what these moments will be like for him later in life. How will he remember this night and the days he spent in the record shop? Marlene's car is across the well-lit street. We're almost close enough to read the license plate.

The sound of a walkie-talkie rises up right beside us. I press myself against the wall, pulling Tom with me. An officer steps out of a building on the other side of the alley. We're in a dark area, but if he turns around and shines his light our way, this will all be over.

The officer says, "Moving north on Percy." We push farther back against the wall. The officer turns and seems to be looking directly at us. Tom's face is partially lit by the nearby streetlight. I try to pull him back, but I can already read his mind. It's all over his face. I shake my head no.

He leans forward.

I pull him back. Mouth *no* again. I feel as if I'm about to cry. Somehow, I thought this part would be the easiest. Walk in, get Ben and Tom, and then leave. That all the other things before would be the hard parts.

Wrong again.

Tom looks down at Ben.

Pushes my hand from his arm.

He's about to step out when the officer's walkie-talkie reports. "Negative. Proceed south on Percy and meet up with C team."

The officer turns and grumbles something before raising the radio to his mouth and saying, "Affirmative."

"Ready?" I say to Tom.

"You two go first," he says. "The fewer of us out at once, the better, right?"

"You'll be right behind us?" I say.

"Yes."

I take another look around the corner, see nothing, grasp Benny a little tighter and run. My legs feel like tree trunks. I stumble a couple of times and begin to wonder if I wasn't more damaged in the car accident than I thought.

When I trip, Benny grabs me tighter.

"It's okay, buddy, we'll get you to your mom," I say.

"I know you will," he whispers in my ear. I lean back from him so I can look at his face. His eyes are all over the place, full of the wonder of being out at night. Every moment for a five-year-old is like the first ever. He'll forget all about what has happened here.

I hope.

We get to the car as a cruiser turns the corner. There's a spotlight on the side, pointed toward the falls. The circle of light is quickly moving toward us, and I can't get the keys out of my pocket fast enough. As I pull them past the lip of my pocket, they catch on something and slip from my hand, crashing to the asphalt.

"Under," I say, setting Ben on the ground. He slides under the car without question. I follow him. We freeze there, huddled together as the cruiser pulls into the parking lot. The spotlight cuts across the car. I pull Ben closer to me. We cannot get caught here, is all I can think. Not now. Not this way.

I see Tom coming out into the light across the street. *No, Tom*, I say to myself. *Go back. Please just go back. It's going to be okay.*

He keeps walking. Not running, just steadily walking toward the cruiser. But then, as quickly as it pulled up, the cruiser tears off, the spotlight jumping around the falls as it goes.

I pull Ben out from beneath the car and unlock the door.

"Get in, buddy," I say, and Ben scrambles inside.

As I'm putting Ben's seat belt on, Tom comes up behind me and says, "Close."

I slam the door. "We have to go."

Tom swings around the front of the car and gets in the passenger seat. As we back out, I think of things to say to him. But everything that comes to mind sounds stupid. What he's done is too kind for words. And he was still willing to do more.

So we drive in silence. I check the rearview mirror over and over again. Ben is looking out the window, then at the ceiling, then playing with his fingers in front of his face.

This isn't exactly how I envisioned the trip. I thought it would be more heroic. More end-of-a-long-journey elation. Instead, I'm just tired, and I feel like crying. It's too late, it's been too long a day, and I'm an emotional wreck.

"Thank you," I say to Tom.

"No problem," he replies.

"Sure," I say. "No problem. No big deal. Just another day in the life of Tom Saunders, international man of awesome."

Tom laughs as we turn onto the Hamford Bridge, which takes us south, out of the city. "I sat there, Laur," he says. "You did all the work."

"Your name has been dragged through the mud again," I say.

"I'll change it," he says. "Like, to Tom Jones."

"Or Engelbert Humperdinck."

"Maybe less elaborate," Tom says. "Richard Taylor."

"Where'd that come from?"

"A surf poster on the wall. He's a tall dude with a million-mile smile," Tom says. "It could give me something to work toward."

"Rich, Rick, Dick," I say. This is ridiculous, I think. But also so very calming. Which is when I realize that Tom is working his magic again. Trying to calm *me* down. To make everything seem normal somehow.

I reach over and take my brother's hand. It's not far, but as we drive off the bridge it seems like I've been driving for days, traveled hundreds of miles. I don't let go of Tom's hand until I have to downshift to turn in to a closed-down gas station.

"Well, Richard Taylor," I say. "Thank you."

"I think I'll go with Rick," he says. "It sounds cool."

Erin's Honda Civic is parked in the shadows of the building, and she is standing beside it, waiting. I slow down and pull in beside her, and she has the back door open and is gathering Ben into her arms before I have fully stopped.

"You're okay, Ben," she says. Ben starts to speak, but Erin hugs him closer. "I missed you so much, big guy."

"Are we going on the adventure now?" Ben says.

I don't know exactly what Erin has told Ben about all of this—how she explained everything that was going to happen. She'd told me she was going to tell him it would be an adventure. She and Tom bought throwaway phones so she could call Ben while he was hiding, but I don't know if that happened.

"Yes," Erin says.

"To the city?"

"To the city," Erin says.

Tom and I get out of the car.

"Do the police have the files?" Erin asks.

"They do," I reply. "They also have Jack. Detective Evans actually brought him in. I sent the files to every newspaper I could think of."

"Will he be charged with anything? Will he go to jail?" Her eyes go round in the dim light.

"I couldn't tell from the files. I didn't have enough time. But it looks pretty bad."

She kisses Ben again. "Jack can talk his way out of anything," she says.

"There's a lot of proof there," I say, trying to reassure her. "There will be an investigation."

Erin nods, but she doesn't seem convinced. After everything she has been through, the years of living with Jack Carter and his lies, it must be difficult to believe she might actually be free.

"People don't like corruption in politics," she says. "These men in power try to help one another out of things like this, but people will hate him." She inhales. "That's almost enough. Thank you. A million times, thank you." She gathers me into a hug, and I hold her tightly. She releases me and walks up to Tom, holding a car key out in front of her. "For you," she says to Tom. Tom takes the key. "It's around the corner. A blue Subaru."

"I can't..."

"You can take this. I have no use for it. I can't drive it, and I don't have time to sell it. If you don't take it, it'll sit right here in this parking lot until someone steals it." She closes Tom's hand around the keys. "Consider it a gift from the mayor for all your hard work and community involvement. You won't be touched by any of this. You've saved us, and I can't think of any way I can ever actually repay you."

"My pleasure," Tom says. She pulls him into an embrace, and they stay that way for a moment.

"Good luck," she says.

"Same to you." She darts around the front of the car to the driver's side. "We have to go," she says. "There's no telling how long it will be before Jack convinces the police to let him go."

"Take care, Ben," I say.

He looks out the window. "You too, Lauren," he says, in his little big-man voice. He holds a pack of Beyblades up. "So cool," he says.

Erin opens the driver's door and gets in.

I lean in the open passenger window. "Will you be back?"

"I don't know," Erin says. "Right now, I plan to. I'm going to send a report to the police, with a picture of Ben and me with a newspaper to show when it was taken and all that. It'll explain that I've fled due to fear for my life. I'll send pictures of my broken arm from last year."

My face must have dropped. "You said—"

"A slip, I know. It wasn't a slip. That was Jack. So were those bruises you saw. I'll send all those photos to the media. But if that doesn't work, I'm ready to disappear."

"I hope I see you again," I say.

"Thank you again, Lauren. I couldn't have done any of this without you." I step away from the car. As she backs out, I wave to Ben. His face is glowing. He's tearing into the package of Beyblades. A moment later, they are nothing but taillights on the highway.

"What happened with Grady?" Tom asks. "Did he find you?"

"He did," I say. "Just like you said he would."

"So where is he?"

"Likely at the police station," I say. "Or the hospital."

"What happened?" Tom says. His face is twisted in concern.

"JJ tried to ram us. Don't worry—he'll be okay."

"You can explain why this all happened the way it did?"

"I can try," I say. And then I do something I haven't done since we were kids. I wrap my arms around my brother and hold on tightly. He feels so different, so much like a man.

"When did you get so big?" he says to me.

"Me! What about you? You need a shave," I say, holding him away from me. "You'd better go."

"Wish me luck," he says. I want to hold on to him and try to make up for all the times I pushed him away. I wish there were a crevice we could walk through and find ourselves ten years in the past. Farther, maybe. I would just need one little shift. One day when I stood up for him.

For myself.

The day my mom sent him away. The day everyone thought he was one thing, and I took the easy route. I went along with them. I let everything I knew about Tom disappear in this fog of speculation and figured I could never know for certain.

Of course I knew.

I knew because Tom told me. He told me what he was doing with that kid. Asking him about a sand castle. That was it.

The relief I felt when he moved across town will stay with me forever. The ease with which a problem disappeared. But he was never a problem. He's my brother.

I feel as though I'm about to cry because everything is coming at me at once.

"I want to go with you," I say.

"I'll be back," he says. "Or...I don't know, I'll send for you. Don't worry—I've gotten pretty good at looking out for myself."

He smiles again, then turns away.

I watch him walk to the car. He presses a button on the fob, and the lights flash.

"Sweet," he says. He turns around one last time before getting in the car. "Until we meet again," he says.

"See you, Rick!"

My cell buzzes. I pull it from my pocket.

Where are you? It's Detective Evans.

On our way.

TWENTY-SEVEN

Detective Evans isn't an idiot.

She's been blinded by her beliefs, certainly.

She's been tricked. She understands that now.

But she's not an idiot.

"You were witnessed leaving the scene of an accident," she says to me. "Where did you go?"

"I went to look for Tom."

"Had your brother contacted you?" she asks. She looks disheveled, which is a first.

"No."

"So where did you go?"

"To the warehouse district."

She shakes her head. "No, you didn't. We have officers there. No one saw you in that area. How did you get there?"

"I borrowed a friend's car," I say.

"Where did you actually go?"

"I just said—" I begin, but she cuts me off.

"Stop lying," she says. "I can't take any more lies. Where is Benjamin Carter?"

"I don't know."

"Where is your brother?"

"I don't know."

"You do know," she says, slamming a fist onto the table. "Where are they?"

"Have you found Joe Fisher?" I ask.

"Where did you get that information?" she demands.

I don't want to lie to her any longer. So I take the only route available to me. "I can't tell you that, and you can't make me. The information is accurate. It's all true. Our mayor has been using his influence for his own financial gain. His son was involved in the death of Michael Brent, the street racer. His daughter is dating a dealer. The Carters are not who everyone thinks they are."

"You said you knew where Tom was. That you would be bringing him in."

"He still might show," I say. "I mean, anything is possible."

"I've passed the place where I ask nicely, Lauren," she says.

What can you say to a statement like that? I give her a little shrug. "The truth is, I don't know."

She reaches out and grabs my phone. She won't find anything on it. I reset it before I drove to the police station.

I also put a password on.

Detective Evans holds the phone out to me.

"Unlock it," she says.

"Why?"

"Do it."

"Why?"

"I want to see what you have been texting your brother. Lauren, this is very serious now."

I decide not to respond. She has completely lost her cool.

"Have you had contact with your brother?" she says.

I don't respond. I don't have to. It's over now.

"Lauren, have you had contact with your brother?"

"You know what? I don't think he's coming, and I'm pretty tired, so I think I'll go home." I stand up. "Sorry it didn't work out for you."

"If you are withholding information, you can be prosecuted," she says.

"What kind of information? What could I possibly know?"

"Where did you get those files?"

"They're real, right?" I drop the USB drives on the desk. "I guess you can have the originals. Every newspaper in the state will be sending people to little Resurrection Falls to see what is going on. There are files in there that could link people much higher up than our mayor. So I would hold on to those if I were you."

"Where did you get them?"

"The truth? Is that what you're actually looking for?"
I lean against the table. "The problem is that your truth is a
bit of a gray area."

"Where did you get these?" she repeats.

"You still can't see that it doesn't matter? All the
numbers you need are on those drives. It goes to show how
powerful the man thought he was that he actually named
files *Bribes*. Do you want to stand behind someone like that?
Do you want to protect that kind of person?"

"They are private property."

"There's a beautiful truth to them," I tell her. "Because no
matter what anyone says, those numbers are real. They were
input into perfect little spreadsheets. Document upon document of information. There are trails you can follow, accounts
you can check and businesses you can investigate. That's all
before you even talk to anyone." I move toward the door, and
Detective Evans doesn't stand. She watches me leave.

TWENTY-EIGHT

SUNDAY

"We couldn't have done it without you," I say again.

Grady isn't happy. I mean, obviously.

"You could have told me," he says.

"I *should* have told you. But we didn't want you to know anything."

He looks at me over the table.

"That sounds bad. It was Tom's idea," I try. But I can't throw Tom under the bus for this one. "We both actually decided it would be better. I mean, Tom knew you more, and he thought that if you knew anything, and you were picked up by the police at any time in the past few days, then you'd have to lie to them."

"Tom was worried about me having to lie to the police?"

"He was." I reach across the table and grab his free hand. Grady's arm is in a sling. He sprained something and has to keep the arm tight to his body. He winces whenever he moves.

"Or was it that you didn't trust me?" Grady says, pulling his hand away.

"We trusted you, Grady. Tom didn't want you to be involved."

"But he expected me to get involved."

I sit back in the booth. It's lunch hour on a sunny Sunday. I've missed two days of school and been bombarded by the media. In hindsight, I wonder if I should have sent the files anonymously. After all, the content of those drives really could speak for itself.

The police aren't officially saying anything beyond the fact that Jack Carter has been held for questioning. But based on what I am hearing, it seems as though an arrest will happen sometime today. They really don't have a choice.

There's a picture of Erin and Ben on the local news site with the caption *We feared for our lives every day* beneath it.

Everything will come out soon enough.

"Why?" Grady says.

"There are a lot of whys, Grady. Which one would you like to delve into first?"

"Why did Erin have to leave this way?"

"Jack was done with her. He already had a younger mistress. Erin has known about it for months but decided not to do anything right away. She wanted to get out of the marriage, but she needed to do it with some dignity, and, I guess, get her revenge."

"Okay," Grady says. He sets his hamburger back on its plate. "Why'd she ask you?"

This is the first time we've been able to speak to one another aside from the odd text. In an attempt to keep Grady entirely out of the spotlight, I'd blocked him out. I had to sneak through my backyard to get downtown. The media have mostly disappeared now, but there are still a couple of journalists keeping vigil outside my house. For what purpose, I have no idea.

I'd said *No comment* at least a thousand times already.

"She didn't—not at first," I explain. "Ben told me his mother was sad. I asked her about it, and she fell apart. Erin and I have known one another for so long that she decided to trust me. She really didn't have anyone else."

"You could have told me," Grady says again. He's moving from angry to pouting.

I can deal with pouting so much more easily.

"Think of it this way," I say. "What could I have possibly told you that would have helped at all?"

"You could have told me about the USB drives. About the corruption. About the fact that your brother *actually had* Ben."

"We didn't know what the corruption was," I say. "Erin knew something was going on. When Joe Fisher showed up in their lives, she noticed that Jack wasn't leaving the house every day just to see his girlfriend. There were more phone calls with men. People sometimes came to the house. She'd also found documents from Jack's lawyer. Jack was going to divorce her and try to gain custody of Ben. That was the tipping point. She couldn't let him have Ben."

"Don't try and tug on my heartstrings," Grady says. "It all could have—"

"What?" I say. I reach out and grab his hand again. "What could have? It all worked out. Everything."

I can't convince him not to feel used. I would feel used in the same situation. I doubted Tom when he suggested that we keep it all from Grady. But I had to trust him.

"Tom knew I would try and find you, didn't he?" Grady says, pulling his hand from mine and pushing his plate away from him.

"He knew you would find me."

"How could he know that?"

"Because he knew you would want to help."

Grady pulls a twenty from his wallet and leaves it on the table as he slides out of the booth. "I have to get out of here," he says.

I follow him outside and, without thinking, take his hand. He doesn't pull away or let go. In fact, I feel his fingers wrap in mine.

"Where is he now?" Grady says, not looking toward me.

"He went to New York," I say. "No one else knows that. Erin has friends who work in theater there, and they have promised to help Tom get a part in a Broadway show.

Or, at least, he can sing in one of the clubs. He's going to try and make it as a singer."

"And he will," Grady says. "Which I guess means that's the end of our band."

"He didn't abandon you, Grady. He helped a woman who was in a terrible situation."

"Yeah," he says. We're in front of Radicals Records. Grady stops. "They were in there the whole time?"

"Yup. Erin took Ben from his room, and Tom drove him down here. Erin had told Jack that her car was in the shop. She'd parked it behind the house, right where we were parked when you hacked their Wi-Fi. Then Tom left the car at the repair shop downtown once he'd gotten Ben into the store."

"Ben must have been so scared," Grady says.

"He's an old soul," I say. "And Tom is great with him. In the past year or so, Tom has spent a lot of time with Ben and me."

We cross the street and walk to a bench by the river.

"Erin had been worried about how Jack treated Ben," I say. "I mean, she wasn't going to stay with Jack anyway, but he's still Ben's father. The problem is that Jack seemed to see his son as an annoyance. Ben wasn't fast enough, strong enough, smart enough. He would never make it as an athlete, or a politician. He was too sensitive and strange. Another failure." I drop to the bench, and Grady sits down beside me.

"She showed me the bruises on her arms from where Jack had grabbed her, twisting her skin when he was angry,"

I explain. "Then she began telling me about the secret meetings Jack had. The conversations she overheard between Jack and some stranger. Then, completely by accident, she bumped the compartment on the bottom of Jack's desk and discovered the USB drive."

"By accident?" Grady says. "My bullshit senses are tingling."

"She was looking for something. I mean, can you imagine living in that house? Knowing your husband was up to something, but not what? Then finding out he was going to divorce you and try to take your child away? You'd spend all your time trying to find something to help you. Some proof that what you were feeling wasn't wrong."

"I'd snoop around his office as well," Grady says. "I guess."

"She tried the drive and, obviously, couldn't get into the contents. The USB drive has the name of the company on it. She looked that up and discovered that there had to be another drive. That she couldn't get into the files without both drives. Which is when she came to me. She didn't expect me to find the other drive. She thought I was good with computers and could get the files anyway."

"That's impossible," Grady says.

"Well, I know that now."

"And that's all you knew before I found you?"

"She had some suspicions about Steph's boyfriend, though what Justin Price did was an open secret around school.

It's just that no one ever dug that deeply or did anything to bring him down. Erin was afraid for Ben. And for herself. With those kinds of people around the house and everything."

"Sure," Grady says. "I can see that."

"The real beginning was when JJ crashed into their house one night, freaking out and wanting to talk to his dad. Erin listened in on that conversation between the two of them, and though she didn't get the whole story, she knew something was going on that was not entirely innocent. She also saw the way Jack behaved toward JJ afterward. As if he no longer existed. Like he'd been written off. The car disappeared, the police report was written, and the news of the other boy's death was released. She put it all together and felt sick. She found it difficult to look at her husband or her stepson. But she couldn't prove anything."

"That's a long time to be in that kind of situation," Grady says.

"She lived like that for almost a year. Wondering what was going to happen next. Feeling helpless to do anything. I guess that's why she came to me."

Grady leans back on the bench. "Okay," he says. "You were trying to protect Erin."

"Yes."

"So you didn't want to tell me what exactly was going on for her sake and my own."

"Yes," I say. "We weren't trying to keep you in the dark. And I hated lying to you."

After a long pause, he says, "I can live with that."

"Can you?"

"Right now I'm just saying it, but one day I might believe it as well."

"Thank you," I say again. Looking at Grady, I can tell it is going to take some time for him to forgive me. If he ever can.

"We've done something great," I say. "You realize that?"

"I guess."

"We've saved a kid from a life of never being quite good enough. We've saved a woman from a marriage she needed to get out of. We've shed light on a corrupt mayor."

"I know," Grady says.

I stand up, and Grady looks at me and smiles. I smile back and say, "That's a good one."

"Thanks," he says, still smiling.

ACKNOWLEDGMENTS

First thanks goes to Sarah Harvey for her immediate enthusiasm for this book. Also to the rest of the team at Orca Book Publishers: Andrew Wooldridge, Leslie Bootle, Dayle Sutherland and everyone else out there on the warm coast who I look forward to actually meeting someday. A very special thanks goes to Robin Stevenson for her amazing edits of this book. I can't say enough about how much hard work Robin put into this to bring its core to the surface.

JEFF ROSS is an award-winning author of seven novels for young adults. He currently teaches scriptwriting and English at Algonquin College in Ottawa, Ontario, where he lives with his wife and two sons. For more information, visit www.jeffrossbooks.com.